Copyright © 2022 by Melody Tyden

Cover design by: GetCovers

A MATTER of TIME

MELODY TYDEN

Chapter One

~**Tonia**~

The big Texas sky stretched out in front of me, as beautiful as ever, but my eyes were fixed firmly on the road as I barreled down the highway. I should have been at the ranch an hour ago already, and if I took much longer to get there, my brother would kill me. For someone who made a living teaching other people how to manage their time, running late didn't look good on me.

Not that it had been my choice to be late. First, my alarm didn't go off that morning. Next, I broke the heel off one of my shoes when I went to throw it in my truck so I had to make an emergency run to the shoe store, and finally, an accident closed my usual route out of Houston. If it were any other day, I'd have said the universe wanted to tell me something and just stayed home instead, but on that particular day, not showing up wasn't an option.

My big brother, Dex, would be marrying the love of his life in less than twenty minutes, and I was supposed to be in the bridal party, as long as I could make it to the ceremony on time.

My phone rang again, no doubt with someone from my family on the other end wondering where in the hell I'd gotten to, but I couldn't stop to answer it. That would only make me later.

With a huge sigh of relief, I finally reached the exit for Sandy Creek, the small town where I grew up. My family's ranch sat on the outskirts of town on the way in, but I drove right past it. The wedding would be taking place at the Armstrong ranch on the other side of town, the family home of Dex's fiancée, Shawna.

Shawna's daddy and my daddy had been rivals as long as any of us could remember, but once Dex and Shawna got together, they agreed to put the past behind them... for the most part. The battle over which ranch would get to host the wedding had been epic, but eventually Shawna's daddy won out, mostly because Dex seemed incapable of saying no to his bride-to-be. Since my daddy behaved just the same way with his wife, Dex could hardly be blamed for that.

Now I just needed to find me a sweet Texas gentleman who would bend over backwards to give me whatever my heart desired; surely, that wouldn't be too much to ask.

At last, I pulled into the long drive past the Armstrong Ranch sign, past the fields and the barns and up to the main house. Built around the same time as most houses in town, the two-storey farmhouse had a wide wrap-around porch and a welcoming, well-kept yard. Guests had already gathered beneath the trees where the chairs had been set up for the ceremony, the aisle strewn with flower petals leading to Italian-style columns holding up an arch in front of a painted backdrop of the Tuscan countryside. Swearing beneath my breath, I quickly threw the truck into park and grabbed my bags from the seat next to me, including my new shoes.

"You're late!" my 18-year-old sister Billie exclaimed as soon as I walked through the front door. The phone in her hand made me guess she'd been the one trying to reach me. "Dex is going to kill you."

I knew that, and dwelling on it wouldn't get me ready any faster. "Where's the bathroom? I've got five minutes to get changed."

She pointed me down the hall before calling out after me: "Three minutes, actually!"

Ignoring her, I raced towards the bathroom door and twisted the doorknob, only to find it locked. With a groan, I banged on the door. "Unless the bride's in there, I'm going to need you to come out right now. Bridesmaid emergency!"

"Hold your horses, I'm almost ready." A male voice answered me, low and rather sexy, and also vaguely familiar.

I wouldn't be put off. "Unless you've got something I ain't never seen before, open up and we can share the space. This is urgent."

The lock clicked, and a second later, the door opened to reveal the last person I expected or wanted to see: my ex-boyfriend, Cameron Bailey. Once upon a time, my stomach would flutter at the sight of him, but even though he'd only gotten better-looking with age, my feelings had definitely changed.

His deep brown eyes looked down at me with their usual smug expression and a teasing smirk pulled at his lips. "Oh, I guarantee you've seen it before, Sugar."

I hardly needed to be reminded of that. Losing her virginity wasn't the kind of thing a woman forgot, and Cam had been my first. Normally, I would have made a smartass response straight back at him, but given my current situation, I didn't have time to trade barbs. "Shove over."

Pushing my way into the bathroom next to him, I pulled my dress out of its bag, glancing at Cam out of the corner of my eye.

"Aren't you a little fancy for sitting in the back row? I didn't even know Dex invited you."

Along with his slicked-back dark hair, he had just finished pulling on the jacket of a tux that could easily pass for one of the groomsmen's suits. It seemed like overkill for a guest, no matter how good it looked on him.

Never in a million years would I admit to anyone that I thought it looked good.

Cam adjusted the sleeves of his jacket as he inspected himself in the mirror. "Shawna invited me, actually, and Dex just heard from Chris

Weston about twenty minutes ago to say he got called in and can't make it. They asked me to step in."

Damn it. Besides being a doctor, Chris was one of Dex and Shawna's best friends. They met two years earlier when Shawna first got her cancer diagnosis and he guided them through the chemotherapy and radiation treatment that got her into remission and healthy enough to be marrying my brother that day. It would have meant a lot to them both for him to be there, but they could hardly complain if other patients needed him at the hospital.

"So, you got called off the bench? Were they that desperate?" As I asked the question, I pulled my shirt up over my head, leaving my long, blonde hair a staticky mess. Time was ticking and I needed to get outside as soon as possible. I couldn't wait any longer for him to leave.

He didn't immediately answer me, and when I looked over to see why not, I could have sworn he'd been staring at me in the mirror, though he quickly looked away when he saw me looking. "Guess I'm the right size for this suit," he said in what he must have meant to be a charming way. I used to find him charming. "Fits me pretty good, don't you think?"

He did a catwalk pose in front of the mirror, and if I were being truthful, he did look damn good, his toned, lean body making the suit look better than it had any right to. I had no intention of complimenting him, though, so I simply glared at him, unimpressed, as I pulled my jeans down. "Nobody's going to be looking at you."

His jaw clenched, just for a moment, before he put his usual smirk back on. "No, I s'pose not, but I will be in the wedding photos now, which means you and me together on Dex and Shawn's mantle, for the rest of time."

I didn't dignify that with a response. "Are you finished yet? I'm kind of in a hurry here."

I bent down to step into my dress, and that time, when I glanced into the mirror, there could be no doubt he'd been watching me, his eyes on my ass.

When he spoke again, his voice sounded tight. "Yeah, I think I'm done, Sugar. See you out there."

He headed out the door and with him finally out of the way, I quickly finished pulling my dress on and touching up my hair and makeup. The pastel yellow dress went well with my blonde hair, which I quickly pulled up into a twist. A bit of eyeliner and mascara brought out my blue eyes, and a pale pink lipstick completed the look, making my lips look plump and sweet. My bladder complained, but I had no time to pee; that would have to wait as I pulled my new shoes on and hurried out the door.

Everyone else had already gathered behind the house, and my mother shot me a disapproving look as I hurried over. "Cutting it a little close, Tonia."

"I know. I'm sorry, but I'm here. I just had a…"

I didn't even finish the sentence as I caught sight of Shawna, looking absolutely stunning in her beautiful white dress. It looked a little big on her since she'd bought it before her latest round of chemo and had lost a lot of weight since then, but she still looked amazing. I could just make out the toes of her cowboy boots peeking out from beneath the skirt.

"Holy hell, Shawna. Dex is going to lose his shit when he sees you!"

"Tonia!" My mom cast an apologetic glance over at Shawna's mother before shaking her head at me. "Can you make it through the ceremony without cussing, please?"

I mimed zipping my lips shut, someone handed me my bouquet, and we were off. Time to get my brother married, once and for all.

~Cam~

All through the ceremony, my gaze kept drifting, entirely of its own accord. The stunning bride looked like pure sunshine with her short blonde hair and her radiant smile. That hair used to be a lot longer before her chemotherapy made it all fall out, but it had started growing back, a reminder of the resilience of life and the power of love. Dex's support for her had never wavered, and now, they got to enjoy their beautiful day together. When they made their vows to each other, not a dry eye could be seen in the place, mine included.

But none of that stopped my eyes from wandering, far more often than I would have liked, to the woman in the pale-yellow bridesmaid's dress, the woman with the bluest eyes I'd ever seen and the loudest mouth too.

I used to think that someday I would marry Tonia Callahan. I pictured a day just like this, underneath the big sky with a light breeze blowing, the smell of manure covered by the fresh flowers all around. I pictured her daddy in his cowboy hat and boots despite wearing a suit and her mama looking proud and maybe a little surprised that Tonia hadn't scared me off. My family would be there too, just as proud as the Callahans but not quite as loud about it, and we'd dance long into the night under the stars.

We might have just been teenagers when we were together, but I loved her, without a doubt, and I had been pretty sure she loved me too.

Once, I couldn't go a day without seeing her, but that day at the wedding marked the first time in months we were breathing the same air. I'd long ago given up any hope of an apology from her, and until she gave me one, we didn't have much else to say to each other. I'd heard she moved to Houston, same as me, but I hadn't run into her there yet. The city was a little different from a place like Sandy Creek: if you wanted to avoid someone, you could.

The ceremony ended with Dex dipping Shawna and kissing her hard and long in front of the crowd as everyone hooted and hollered their approval, and as they walked together back down the aisle, I held out my arm to Tonia. Somehow, it worked out that the guy I replaced had been the one paired with her in the bridal party, which meant us walking down the aisle together and sharing a dance later too.

God sure had a strange sense of humour sometimes.

Somewhat to my surprise, she took my arm without complaint. It seemed even she wouldn't go so far as to carry her grudge into her brother's wedding, though I wouldn't have put money on that being the case. As soon as we reached the end of the aisle, she dropped my arm like it scalded her and headed over to her mama and sisters, while I made my way quickly to the bride and groom to shake their hands.

"Congratulations, you two. This must be just about the prettiest wedding I ever saw."

I meant that sincerely, not exaggerating in the least. As an artist, Dex had created the beautiful backdrop of rolling hills and cypress trees himself. Shawna had dreamed of getting married in Italy, but with all the money they'd spent on her cancer treatment, it hadn't been possible. Since they couldn't go to Italy, Dex had brought Italy to her.

"Thank you, Cam." He couldn't stop grinning as he shook my hand firmly. Obviously, he felt pretty good about how it went too. "And thanks for stepping in at the last minute, we really appreciate it."

"My pleasure."

In a different life, I could have been part of this wedding all along. Dex and I had gotten along well back in high school when Tonia and I were dating. We might have even become good friends if Tonia and I stayed together, but when we split, Dex made it clear where his loyalties lay.

"I like you, Cam," he told me apologetically at the time. "But if Tonia finds out I'm still hanging out with you, she'll castrate me, and I'm kinda attached to all my parts."

I had no comeback for that, since I knew just how hot Tonia's temper could get. Hard not to be aware of it when it had been responsible for our break-up in the first place. "I understand. Hopefully it'll all blow over soon anyway, once she realizes she's being unreasonable."

That had been wishful thinking on my part, obviously. There we were, almost five years later, and nothing had blown over other than my hopes of any kind of reconciliation.

Tables were brought out for the buffet dinner, and no one had assigned seats, so I sat with some old high school friends, catching up with what everyone had been up to until the time came to start the dance. The sun had just started to go down, casting long shadows over the whole scene, making it look even more romantic as Dex and Shawna shared their first dance.

When the song ended, they invited the rest of the bridal party to join them, and I held out my hand to Tonia once more. Her hand rested lightly on my shoulder as mine circled around her waist, both of us relaxing into an easy two-step. The live band and the happy chatter of the guests filled the air around us, and her hair still smelled like flowers when I inhaled; I had no idea what kind of flowers, but the same scent it had always had. She must still use the same shampoo. No one could say that Tonia wasn't loyal when she found something she decided would be worth holding onto.

"So, you live in Houston now?" she asked after almost a minute of awkward silence. I had just been starting to wonder if we were going to make it through the whole song without saying a word.

"Yup." I planned to stick to answering only the question she asked. "You do too, I hear."

"Yup." She repeated it in exactly the same tone I'd used, obviously mocking me, and I had to shake my head, which she didn't appreciate. "What's that smirk for?"

I raised my eyebrows at her. "I didn't smirk."

"You did," she argued. "Your lips did that thing they do when you think you're being clever about something. I know what I saw."

"You think you know better than me what my own face is doing?" I knew she thought exactly that, and she didn't disappoint me.

"I'm the one looking at it," she pointed out. "Whether you meant to or not, that's what you did."

"Well, you're the queen of deciding what other people's actions mean, after all."

I expected that to put a stop to her argument, which it did, but I didn't expect her to stop dancing too. We ground awkwardly to a halt as she planted her feet firmly on the ground.

"Keep moving, Sugar," I said through gritted teeth, trying to keep smiling as people began to notice us standing stock still in the middle of the dance floor. "The dance ain't over yet."

"Oh, yes, it is."

Twisting out of my arms, she stormed off the dance floor, leaving me to shoot an apologetic smile in the direction of the bride and groom before taking off after her.

"Tonia." I hissed her name, trying to keep my voice down as she pushed her way past the people gathered and headed down the dirt road that led away from the house towards the back fields. "Where are you going?"

"Far away from you." The words were thrown back over her shoulder as she didn't even turn around to talk to me.

Luckily, no matter how angry she might be, she was still wearing her heels, so it didn't take much for me to catch up to her. I grabbed onto her arm to halt her progress. "Come on, stop. You really want to make a scene at your brother's wedding?"

"Don't tell me how to feel, Cam." Her eyes were full of defiance as she tried to pull away from me, but I held her firmly.

"I'm not. I'm telling you how to act, since apparently you still haven't grown up enough to figure it out on your own."

I really should have seen that slap coming, but she managed to catch me by surprise anyway, and my face burned where her palm connected with it.

Shit, that really stung.

"Nothing in my life is any of your business, and it hasn't been for the last five years. You've done your duty today, played the shining knight as usual, so why don't you disappear now and let me enjoy the rest of the night with my family? They're the people I actually came here to see."

If she thought she could hurt my feelings, she was mistaken. "Fine with me. I didn't actually come here to see you either. Not everything is about you, Tonia."

I turned around and began to walk away, but I knew she wouldn't let that go. She always had to get the last word in, no matter what, and once again, she didn't disappoint.

"Maybe Marley Stevens is at home tonight. You could always go over there."

Of course she went there. It always came back to that. Though my eyes closed and my jaw clenched, I still had my back to her and I didn't stop walking, so from her point of view, it shouldn't look like those words had gotten to me at all.

That was the one good thing about the whole damn mess: Tonia never knew just how bad she broke my heart, and I'd be damned if I would give it away now.

Chapter Two

Six months later

~Tonia~

The click of my high heels sounded confident and poised as I strode across the lobby of the high-rise office tower in downtown Houston. My laptop bag slung over my shoulder carried not only my computer but all of the worksheets and handouts I needed for my presentation that day. My blonde hair had been neatly straightened, my makeup looked understated and professional, and my dress was a perfect mix of polished and sexy. The golden hue complemented my colouring and the cut of the fabric highlighted my curves without being too showy about it. My sister, Laura, had helped me pick it out; despite being a country girl through-and-through, she had the best eye for fashion of anyone in the family, and when I told her I needed a few pieces to help me look the part for work, she had been happy to lend a hand. As I caught a glimpse of my reflection in the window, I could tell she'd absolutely nailed it.

Anyone who saw me would think I looked calm and cool and completely in control. No one would be able to guess just how fast my heart beat as I went up to the reception desk with a smile on my face.

"Good morning, I'm here to see Jason Barnly at Barnly Oil."

The man's eyes widened just slightly in appreciation as he took me in, confirming my suspicions about how good I looked. "Name?"

"Tonia Callahan from A Matter of Time."

He placed a call and told me someone would be down to meet me in a minute, so I stepped away and took a quick look around. The building appeared shiny and new, just like the business I'd come there to help, and just like my own business too.

I launched A Matter of Time just over a year earlier, but it had been brewing in my head for a long time before that. I always planned to run my own business so I studied business management at college, but when I graduated, I still hadn't decided exactly what kind of business I wanted to get into. I needed something I felt passionate about to make it a success, but the products and services I looked into didn't excite me nearly as much as the business of business itself. Organizing, prioritizing, and making each minute count; those were my passions, and after thinking it over for a while, I realized there was no reason I couldn't make *that* my business.

All over the state, there were people with great ideas who didn't know how to use their time effectively. I could help them with that, and with my guidance, they could truly make their businesses bloom.

My brother, Dex, said it came down to me enjoying the chance to tell people what to do, but that only accounted for part of it. I truly got a thrill out of making a difference, out of seeing people put my suggestions into practice and seeing the success that came out of that.

Up until that point, I had been relying on word of mouth to get my name out there. Friends recommended me at first, and when those clients were satisfied, they recommended me to their acquaintances too. Work had been steady for the past year, but I still hoped to get one big breakout job, one that would launch me to the next level, and as I stood in the sleek downtown office building, I had a feeling I had found it.

Houston had hundreds of oil and oil-related businesses and Barnly Oil was a brand-new startup with an excellent pedigree. The owner and

CEO was the son of one of Texas' most successful oilfield suppliers, and he also happened to be a good friend of the real estate manager whose business I had transformed a couple of months earlier. When Jason hired his management team, he mentioned to that friend that he wanted to get them set up properly right from the start so he wouldn't have to unteach any bad habits later on, and his friend had recommended me.

Jason hired me for a whole month on a consultancy basis, to work with each of his executives as a team and one-on-one, and that morning would be my initial presentation to them, a chance to start everything off on the right foot.

If it went well, Jason could spread the word to other businesses in the oil industry, and I might be able to expand my business, to hire more people just like me, and make it the success I had dreamed of.

I *really* wanted it to go well.

I hadn't been provided with the names of the rest of the team and with the company being so new, that information hadn't been made public yet, so I didn't know exactly what the other members of the team were like. However, Jason was young and ambitious, and male, of course, and based on the overall demographics of executives within the oil business, I assumed most of the others were men too. For that reason, I made sure I looked as good as I could that morning. Men paid more attention to women they found attractive; sexist, maybe, but also true, and a fact that I intended to take advantage of. I wanted to have them eating out of the palm of my hand and ready to do everything I told them to do.

"Ms Callahan?" The voice came from a young, pretty woman in a white blouse and red skirt, with dark brown hair and a bright, white smile. She was probably around the same age as me, in her early 20s. "I'm Marianne, Mr Barnly's assistant. Please, come with me."

I would have bet any money on the fact that he'd have a young, pretty assistant. So far, it seemed my assumptions about the business were spot-on.

"Have you known Mr Barnly for long?" I asked her as we got into the elevator together.

Marianne shook her head. "I just started last week. Everything's still pretty new."

I expected that too, and it pleased me to know I was on the right track. The plan I'd put together should be perfect.

"He's really nice," she offered without me having to ask. "They all are. I had a few qualms about working in an office full of men, but so far, they've all been completely appropriate."

That didn't seem like a particularly high bar to clear. If anyone ever dared to be anything less than appropriate with me, they would live to regret it.

The elevator stopped on the 8th floor and we exited into a hallway with several different companies all sharing the same floor. I took a mental note of some of the other business names as we walked past them so I could look them up later and see if they needed my help too. At the end of the hall, we reached the door marked Barnly Oil, where Marianne scanned her employee card and held the door open for me.

Inside, the office space formed a large rectangle with offices around the outside and an open-plan meeting and work station area in the middle. The hum of voices drifted out to us from some of the offices, but no one could be seen from where we stood. The work day hadn't officially started yet.

A larger meeting room took up the left wall, and Marianne led me into it. "You can get set up in here. The team will all be in by nine o'clock. Can I get you a coffee or anything?"

"Yes, please. Black."

Left on my own, I took a closer look around the room. Ten chairs were arranged around the table, but only six people made up the executive team, so I took four of the chairs away so that they would have no choice but to sit close to the front and close to me. That would help make sure I had their undivided attention. After getting my laptop and projector set up, I pulled out my neatly organized handout folders, placing one at each chair along with my personalized pens. Those were my favourite little marketing tools. Every time my clients used them, I wanted them to remember me and how much my training had helped them.

The coffee Marianne brought me quickly disappeared as I got everything set up just right, and I still had fifteen minutes before my scheduled start time. Perfect timing, as usual, and just enough time for me to take a quick trip to the restroom before the attendees started to arrive.

When I returned to the main office, Marianne had sat down at a desk outside what must be Jason Barnly's office with its door closed. She told me where to find the restroom, back down the hallway towards the elevator, and I quickly slipped out and made my way there. It appeared to be one door that led to both the men's and women's, so I pushed it open firmly as I approached, and pushed it directly into the foot of the man standing on the other side, on his way out.

"I'm sorry," I quickly apologized as he muttered a curse under his breath, his head bowed to look down at his foot in his black leather shoes.

He didn't have a suit jacket on, but his pressed white shirt and tie still projected an air of professionalism while giving the impression of a rather firm and attractive body, I couldn't help noticing. Just because I had my business hat on didn't make me blind.

But when he raised his head, my stomach dropped in surprise and confusion.

"Cam? What are you doing here?"

I hadn't seen my ex-boyfriend since the night of Dex's wedding, since I slapped him across his face, and I certainly hadn't expected to run into him in that building of all places, on a morning when I definitely needed to be at the top of my game.

His usual smirk spread across his face as he took me in. "Well, hey there, Sugar. I'd say it was good to see you, if you hadn't just tried to break my toe."

"I didn't..." I started to protest before taking a breath. He wanted to rile me up, as he always did, and I didn't need that. Arguing with him wouldn't do me any good, especially since I was at fault. I could take responsibility for this. "I didn't see you there and I should have opened the door more slowly."

His eyebrows shot up in surprise. "Was that almost a Tonia Callahan apology? Has hell frozen over and everyone forgot to tell me?"

"I'm in a bit of a hurry," I told him, refusing to engage in our usual game of insults. "I imagine you're busy too."

In my mind, I quickly scanned through the business names I had noticed on the doors earlier, wondering which of them he worked for, and just as quickly, I shook the thought out of my head. I really didn't care.

"Always busy," he confirmed, stepping out of the way so I could go past him. There were separate doors to the men's and women's restrooms just inside. "Have a good day, Sugar."

"You can call me Tonia," I corrected, but he had already headed out the door, and if he heard me, he didn't respond.

I used to love when he called me Sugar, his voice growling and low. He told me that he chose that pet name for me because I tasted so sweet. Now, on the rare occasions we ran into each other, he always said it sarcastically, and the last thing I wanted was for anyone from Barnly Oil to hear him speaking to me that way. I needed their respect.

When I had finished and double checked that everything about my appearance remained perfectly in place, I returned to the Barnly Oil office which had grown much livelier in my absence. A couple of people had already taken a seat in the meeting room, and I gave them a warm smile as I walked in, making small talk about the weather and the traffic while we waited for the others to join us. As I expected, both of the early arrivals were young and male, and so were the next two people who entered. One of the remaining empty seats belonged to Jason Barnly himself, so that left only one person who might potentially surprise me.

And surprise me he did when he walked in with the CEO, laughing light-heartedly in that very familiar way of his. Young and male certainly described him, just as I expected.

What I *hadn't* expected was for him to be Cameron Freaking Bailey.

~Cam~

As I got back to my new office, my sore toe throbbed where the door had hit it, but the thoughts swirling around my head were the bigger distraction. What were the odds of running into Tonia here? Did she work here in this building? On this floor? The odds of it seemed astronomical.

She looked incredibly good today, I had to admit, and smelled just as good too. Shoot, why did she have to smell so good? She had always been just my type, before I even knew what a type was, and time had done nothing to change that. I'd been doing so well at putting her behind me, and I forced myself to put her out of my mind again as I said hello to Jason's assistant. Marianne was her name, I believed. Everything here was still new, but this job was a huge opportunity for me, and I'd be damned if I let Tonia get in my head the way she usually did.

"Come on in, Cam," Jason called out from his desk as he saw me in the doorway. "Just the guy I wanted to see."

"Is that good news or bad news?" I joked as I walked in and took a seat across from him. Jason was a friend of a friend of a friend, which was how I found out about the job opening in his new company, and I couldn't be more thrilled to get in on the ground floor of a new startup. I didn't know a thing about oil; unlike some of my classmates in high school, I'd never worked on the rigs in the counties surrounding us. I did know finance, though, and Jason had been impressed enough that he hired me to oversee his new finance department.

Most people my age with my educational background were getting jobs in big banks or investment firms, starting out as small fish in a big pool, hoping that by the time they got to their 40s or 50s, they'd have swum their way to the top. Me, I wanted to start big, so I'd been looking for a small company that would take a risk on a guy like me, and Barnly Oil seemed like a perfect fit. The other members of the management team were almost all my age and we were all eager to work hard and make the business as much of a success as it could be.

Jason took it seriously too, which was why he'd hired this consultant to come in and make sure that we were all making the best use of our time. When one of the other guys on the team wondered if it wouldn't be better to just use the time we were going to spend with this consultant on doing actual work, Jason quickly shut him down.

"This is an investment in our company, and in you. The time you spend now in learning how to organize yourself properly is going to pay off in the long run, and that's what we're all interested in: the big picture."

None of us could argue with that.

"It's nothing bad," he assured me as I settled into the seat in front of his desk. "And maybe this is out of line, I don't know, since I don't know you all that well yet, but everyone who does know you says what a good guy you are, and, well, I could just use some impartial advice."

He'd completely lost me. "Advice about what?"

"About a woman," he admitted sheepishly, glancing over at the closed door as if to double check no one could overhear us.

I definitely hadn't been expecting that, and I couldn't imagine what he'd been told about me that made him think I would be the right one to come to with that kind of question. My track record with the opposite sex was hardly anything to write home about.

"A woman," I repeated, trying to keep my voice free of any kind of judgement. "Is this business-related?"

"Well, that's the issue. You see, she's someone I'm going to be working with, and I don't want to do anything that could come across as sleazy, especially since I'm kind of her boss."

"You're kind of everyone's boss," I reminded him, trying to put him at ease. He obviously felt a little uncomfortable talking to me about this, and although it surprised me that he'd chosen me to confide in, I took it as a good sign too. Being friendly with the boss was never a bad thing.

"Yeah, I guess I am," he agreed, looking relieved at my response, which made me more confident that it had been the right thing to say. "This is all new to me, both being the boss and being interested in someone I work with. I just don't want to screw it up, either with her or for the business. I need to set a good example, you know? Maybe I should just forget the whole thing, but she's really kinda special."

The plaintive expression on his face hit close to home; the poor guy had it bad.

"Well, because you're the boss, it's up to you to set the policy on workplace relationships," I pointed out. "If you say it's okay, then it's okay, as long as you keep it professional while in the office."

"I guess you're right," he agreed hopefully. "Now I just gotta figure out how to find out if she's interested without coming across as a creep."

That made me laugh. "I am definitely not the guy to help you with that."

He smiled too. "Don't worry, I won't get you any more involved than you are already, but thanks for letting me talk that out."

"Anytime." I meant it too; I hoped we could become friends as well as colleagues.

A calendar reminder beeped on his computer and he glanced over at the clock. "Shoot, nine o'clock already. You ready to get started on this time management thing?"

"Sounds like you need it more than me," I teased him as we headed out together to the meeting room. We were still joking back and forth as we walked into the meeting room, until I laid eyes on the woman at the front of the room and the laughter died in my throat.

No way. No *freaking* way was Tonia Callahan standing in my meeting room on my first full day at my new job.

The expression on her face, looking momentarily like a deer caught in the headlights, made it abundantly clear to me that she hadn't known I would be here either. She had seemed genuinely surprised to run into me, quite literally, in the hallway earlier. It didn't feel like an act on her part.

I could call it a joke, certainly, some kind of cosmic prank, but not an act.

"Good morning, Tonia," Jason said, going up to the front of the room and shaking her hand, completely oblivious to my reaction as I sank down into one of the remaining empty seats, trying to swallow even though my mouth had gone completely dry.

Distractedly, I picked up the pen in front of me, trying to find something to keep my hands busy, but quickly dropped it as I realized it had her name on it.

"Gentlemen, this here's Tonia Callahan," Jason told us all. "She's going to whip us all into shape and get this place running like a well-oiled machine, pun intended."

Everyone chuckled politely, including me, though my mouth was still drier than the Chihuahuan desert.

"We're in your hands, Tonia," Jason concluded, giving her a warm smile as he came and took a seat next to me, and a new and entirely unwelcome thought suddenly came to me.

Was *she* the one he'd been talking to me about? He'd said he was 'kind of' the woman's boss, which made sense for someone like Tonia who had come here as an external consultant.

Did I just encourage my boss to hit on my ex-girlfriend?

It took all my self-control not to groan out loud as the thought crossed my mind. Honestly, I thought I was a pretty decent guy overall, just as Jason said. What on earth had I done to deserve this?

~Tonia~

Cam didn't acknowledge me in any way when Jason Barnly introduced me to the team, so I didn't give him any kind of special attention either. For the next two hours, I laid out my program for the team, explaining what I'd be working with them on over the month and what they could expect to have learned by the end of our time together.

Other than a few general training sessions like the one we were in, most of my work would be on a one-to-one basis. I needed to see what kind of organizational system they had in place already, where their strengths and weaknesses were, and build on that together. There were no one-size-fits-all solutions here. My services were completely individualized, letting me truly get to know the people that I had come there to help, and making them the best version of themselves they could be rather than trying to make them into something that felt unnatural for them.

That approach was what made me so good at my job.

Unfortunately, it also meant that I would need to spend several days over the next month *alone* with Cam. From the way his jaw tightened as I laid out the schedule, I could tell he picked up on that too, and that he felt just about as happy about it as I did.

He didn't have to be happy about it though. He could hate every minute of it if he wanted to, just as long as he did what I said and he didn't use our past as an excuse to try to sabotage what I wanted to accomplish.

Would he stoop to that level? I really didn't know, and that worried me. The Cam I used to know had never been cruel or hurtful, but the Cam in front of me, the one with the confident look in his brown eyes, the stubble on his chin, wearing a tie and sitting around an executive's table, wasn't the boy I fell in love with. He had definitely changed; the question remained just how much.

As my presentation drew to a close, I summed up my program as I always did: "I know it sounds like a lot of work, gentlemen, but I guarantee you that in a month, you'll be wondering how you ever wasted so much time before. It's not a question of 'if' I can help you; it's simply a matter of time."

Giving me a nod of approval and a warm smile, Jason started to clap and the other men quickly joined in, following their boss' lead.

"Any questions?" I asked as the applause died off.

One of the men raised his hand, as though we were in school. "I don't spend a lot of time in the office, I'm usually travelling between plants, so it might be a bit tricky for us to coordinate this training."

Jason had already warned me about that. "That's fine. I'm happy to tag along with you for a day or two and we can look at how you can turn those travelling hours into productive work time as well."

"Can you help us get our personal lives in order too?" another man piped up, making the whole room laugh.

"I know you're joking, but the truth is that I can," I replied when they had quietened down again. "When your work day is more efficient, you'll be better able to switch off at the end of the day and truly enjoy your leisure time too. Finding that work-life balance is important to Barnly Oil, and I can definitely help with that."

Jason gave me another nod of approval, clearly pleased with that response.

"Tonia's going to be sending us all calendar invites to make sure we get the time booked in that she needs, and you're expected to accept those. If you need to move other things around, do it. If you can't, just let her know. Anything else for now, Tonia?"

I shook my head. "If there are no more questions, you're all free to go. No point in making a meeting longer than it has to be; that's lesson number one."

They all smiled again and as the meeting broke up, each of them came up to shake my hand and introduce themselves quickly afterwards.

My heart beat a little faster as Cam reached the front of the line. "Cam Bailey," he said, holding out his hand with that typical little smirk on his lips. "Sounds like you got your work cut out for you with this group, Ms Callahan."

So, we were playing it like that, were we? With Jason still in the room, chatting with someone else but potentially listening to us anyway, it seemed clear that Cam didn't want him to know that we already knew each other. I had no problem with that. "I can handle men like you, Mr Bailey. You don't have to worry about me."

That smirk tightened for just a second. "I'm sure I don't. I'll look forward to our first meeting, then."

"Likewise."

When he stepped away, Jason came over next. "That was great, Tonia. I don't know about these guys, but I'm all fired up now, can't wait to get started. If you don't have plans right away, could I tempt you with a lunch offer so we can go over a few things?"

From the corner of my eye, I saw Cam's shoulders stiffen as he picked up his papers from the table.

"That sounds great, Mr Barnly. I'd love to."

"Call me Jason, please," he insisted. "We're going to be seeing a lot of each other over the next month, and Mr Barnly will get old really fast."

I gave him a warm smile. "Sounds good to me, Jason."

One of my pens clattered to the floor, making us both turn just in time to see Cam stooping to pick it up. He glanced back over at us as he stood upright again. "Slipped outta my hand," he explained, gesturing to the pen, and without another word, he walked out of the room.

"I've got a few things I need to do first," Jason told me once Cam had gone. "Meet me in an hour at Tony's?"

"It's a date." We smiled at each other once more as he headed back to his office. Left on my own again, I looked around the empty room, exhaling in relief.

That had gone well. If it weren't for the unexpected surprise of Cam turning up, it would have been pretty much perfect. I just had to make it through the next thirty days without strangling him, and everything would be absolutely fine.

Chapter Three

~**Cam**~

From my office, I could see the main office door, and my eyes kept drifting to it, unintentionally, as I waited for Jason to get back from his lunch with Tonia.

Why did I care? I *didn't* care. I knew she dated other men, and I dated other women too. At that particular point in time, I was single, but I'd been in several other relationships since we broke up. If she or anyone else thought I had been sitting around pining after her for almost six years, they were delusional.

Some of those six years, maybe, but definitely not all of them.

So, if she and Jason were to start dating, it wouldn't be a big deal. Sure, it might be awkward to see her at social occasions after work, but I could handle it. He could put his arm around her and I'd be okay with that. If he kissed her in front of me...

My stomach twisted, but I pushed through it, telling myself to toughen up. That would be okay too. Hell, they could get married for all I care. It really had nothing to do with me. We were never getting back together, so she could date or marry whoever she wanted.

By the time Jason finally got back, my imagination already had them living in a big house in River Oaks with three kids.

I gave him a friendly smile from my desk as he looked in my direction, trying to make it clear that he could talk to me if he wanted to, but he simply gave me a nod and went into his office instead, closing the door behind him and leaving me with absolutely no idea what happened between them.

Frustrated with myself for letting the situation distract me, I did my best to focus back on my work. I had plenty to keep me occupied, and I managed to do a pretty good job of it too until Tonia's name started popping up in my inbox. Along with invitations for our one-on-one training sessions, she also sent me a personalized note; personalized in the very loosest form of the phrase, anyway:

Mr Bailey, I'm looking forward to our time together. If you have any questions before we get started, you can reach me at ...

Obviously, she'd just cut and pasted it, not even taking a second to acknowledge that I might be any different to her from the other members of the team, just like she hadn't said anything to me in the meeting. During the whole presentation, she never avoided looking at me nor looked at me too much. She gave me exactly the same amount of attention that she gave everyone else, so when I went to say hi to her afterwards, I decided to be a smartass and introduce myself since she didn't seem to want to admit we had any kind of past.

I expected her to laugh at me or tell me off for being an idiot, but she didn't. She shook my hand in her confident, assured way, still pretending that we'd never met before, and then she agreed to go for lunch with Jason right in front of me.

Which was fine. I was fine with it. I was.

I kept reminding myself of that as I made my way home after work. A year earlier, I moved into an apartment downtown, right in the heart of the city. Getting a house in the suburbs at that point in my life seemed pointless when I had no one to go home to at the end of the day. It made more sense to be close to work and the nightlife, and my one-bedroom apartment perfectly suited a young, single man like me.

The building had a gym and a pool downstairs, and several of my single, female neighbours flirted with me when I made use of them, but though I flirted back, I didn't go any further than that. The pitfalls of getting involved with someone I couldn't avoid if things went bad seemed too risky; I had definitely had enough of that for one lifetime.

With nothing planned for the evening, I made myself a quick dinner in the kitchen that made up half my living space and ate my meal sitting alone at the counter, reviewing a few more emails from work on my phone. After I finished washing the dishes, I thought I might kick back with a beer in front of the game and zone out to take my mind off things, but even those meagre plans were quickly thwarted as my phone rang and I saw the name that flashed across the screen.

Marley Stevens.

How ironic, considering how Tonia had been on my mind all day. I might as well invite the whole town of Sandy Creek to join her.

"Hey Marley, what's up?"

Holding my phone with one hand, I grabbed my beer with the other and got settled on the couch. Our calls were never short, but to my surprise, it seemed she actually called to talk about me.

"I heard Tonia's working with you now," she opened. "Is that weird?"

"How the hell did you hear that already?" Sure, Sandy Creek was one of those places where everyone knew everyone's business, but even by those standards, that news had spread ridiculously fast.

"Tonia told Dex, who told Shawna, who told Barbara, who told Graham, who told me."

That sounded about right. Even in my apartment in Houston, I couldn't hide from small town gossip.

"Well, sounds like the story got warped along the way. She ain't working with me. She's just doing some consulting work on a temporary basis and then she'll be moving on. We can put up with each other for that long."

"Are you sure you don't want me to talk to her? If I told her exactly what happened..."

"No." I cut her off just as I always did. She'd made that offer before and I always turned her down for the same reason. "She didn't want to hear me out then so she doesn't get to hear about it now."

"You're just as stubborn as she is," Marley pointed out. "One of you has to bend first."

"That's assuming there's something worth bending for. It's all water under the bridge, a bridge that's been burned to the ground. There's no way of going back." The metaphors might be mixed, but I'd made my point.

Even if she understood me, that answer didn't satisfy Marley. "Then why do you two still wind each other up so much? If there's nothing there, it shouldn't bother either of you to be working together. But she's complaining to her brother and you sound like you're ready to crush that beer bottle in your hand, you're wound so tight."

With a frown, I glanced down at the beer in my hand which I was, in fact, holding onto a little tighter than absolutely necessary. Was I really that predictable?

"It's not your problem, Marley," was the only thing I could say in response. "We're all grown-ups now, we can deal with the choices we've made."

"But it's not fair. You shouldn't have to suffer just because you were trying to..."

"I'm not suffering," I countered, interrupting her again. "I'm perfectly happy. I've got a great job, I've got a great apartment in the city, I'm living the life I always wanted. Now, can we talk about something else please? *Anything* else? How's your dad?"

That distracted her, as it always did, and as I got caught up with her latest family drama, I managed to not think about Tonia for the next half hour at least.

When the day finally ended and I laid down in my bed, I mentally checked the date off in the new calendar I'd created in my head: days I might run into Tonia in the office.

One day down, thirty more to go.

~Tonia~

The next few days in the Barnly Oil office went pretty well. Jason told me we could save his one-on-one sessions until the end of the month since he thought it would be more important for me to meet with the other members of the team first. With that in mind, I started with the head of HR, working with him for two days before moving onto the man in charge of engineering, the one whose work took place mostly out of the office. I considered that a bonus since it meant no chance of randomly running into Cam on the way to the restroom, or anywhere else.

"Maybe it's some kind of sign," my brother, Dex, teased me when he and I went out for drinks after my first day at Barnly Oil and I told him about Cam working there.

"A sign that the universe hates me?" I guessed, taking a sip of my martini. Normally, beer and jeans were more my style, but still wearing my dress from the office, I had ordered a drink to match.

Dex, on the other hand, sat there in his usual jeans and t-shirt, having come straight from his workshop, which explained the paint stains on his fingers. He and his wife, Shawna, were in the middle of setting up his brand-new gallery space to sell his artwork. They'd found a small storefront in a slightly run-down area of downtown, the location being the only reason they could afford it. Even so, he would be paying off the mortgage on it for years, not to mention the one on the house they'd bought together too.

He'd always been the more optimistic one between us, trusting that things would work themselves out. I liked to keep tighter control. I wouldn't even think about buying a house until my business was much more settled and I had a lot more money in the bank. Until then, I rented a small apartment and put away as much as I could each month.

Things had a way of going wrong, even when something looked like a sure thing. Experience had taught me that, and I wouldn't let myself get caught out again.

Dex grinned at me as he took a swig of his beer. "Well, Lord knows the universe has a few reasons to hate you, but in this case, I think it's just a sign that this feud between you and Cam has gone on long enough. Time to let bygones be bygones."

"That's what I've been doing," I pointed out. "I've let him live his life and I'm living mine. I don't wish him any kind of misfortune, I just don't want to have to see him every day. Is that too much to ask?"

"There's a difference between forgetting and forgiving," my stubborn brother countered. "You may be able to put him out of your mind when you're not together, but as soon as you see him, you're that hurt and defensive 18-year-old girl all over again. I really think you guys just need to sit down and have an honest talk about the whole thing. Something's gotta give, Tonia, before you go storming off any more dance floors."

That was the first time Dex brought up what happened at his wedding, and it managed to make me blush, no small feat in itself. "Fine, you might have a point. But I really can't help it, I see him and I just want to slap him. It's out of my control."

I gave the most innocent shrug I could, but Dex shook his head at me. "Sounds to me like what you really wanna do is make him hurt like he hurt you. Maybe if you'd've ever told him that, it wouldn't hurt so bad anymore."

I really hated when he made sense. Having grown up with three sisters, my brother had a unique insight into the female psyche, and sometimes, it really annoyed me. "You know, Dex, sometimes a woman just wants to complain, she's not actually looking for solutions."

"Then you've come to the wrong guy," he said with a laugh. "I've got an answer for everything."

That might not be true, but he did always have my back, which I appreciated even when he teased me.

"Now, what's the deal with this Jason Barnly fella?" he asked next, recognizing that I was ready to move the conversation on from talking about Cam. "Was this lunch of yours all business?"

I'd already told him briefly about Jason taking me to lunch, and I couldn't add much more than that. "We chatted a bit about our backgrounds, but it all stayed pretty professional."

"And do you want to keep things professional?" he pressed.

I had a tougher time answering that question. On the surface, Jason should be exactly the kind of guy I would be interested in: smart, ambitious and attractive. He had just enough Texan charm without being over-the-top about it. No one I'd spoken to before taking the job had a bad word to say about him.

So, what held me back? I didn't love the idea of mixing business and pleasure, for one. I didn't want there to be any rumours about me being anything less than strictly professional when it came to the workplace.

But more than that, if I were to be totally honest with myself, Cam himself made me hesitate. I already knew that Jason and Cam were colleagues, and for all I knew, they were friends as well. I didn't need to mix my life up with his anymore than it already had been.

"I'm not sure Jason's looking for anything else," I told my brother. "There's no point in obsessing about it unless he makes a move. You know I don't waste time on indecisive people."

"Oh, I know. But I think you might want to put some thought into it anyway, so you know what you want before you're put on the spot."

Dex didn't usually stick his nose into my love life; the opposite was far more likely to be true. The fact that he felt he should say something let me know that he genuinely wanted to look out for me, and I did my best to reassure him. "Trust me, Dex. I can handle Jason Barnly, or Cam Bailey, or any of the other men at Barnly Oil. You don't need to worry about me."

I truly believed that too, so I had no worries about heading out of town with the head of engineering on Friday morning. He had a visit planned to their processing plant south of Corpus Christi and had invited me along, so I had already planned out exactly how we could use the travelling time to get his schedule whipped into shape. It would be the perfect end to a good first week at Barnly Oil, and the following week, I could take on dealing with Cam.

I had everything completely under control.

~**Cam**~

The office seemed to be Tonia-free on Friday morning, thankfully, and I could relax as I sat down behind my desk. I had done a pretty good job of avoiding her since the meeting on Monday, but I could often hear her voice carrying out from another room while she talked to someone else. She had a way of standing out in a crowd, she always had, and it made it difficult to concentrate when my mind kept drifting back to the past every time I heard her laugh.

Back to the days when I would have done just about anything to make her laugh.

That morning, however, it looked like she wouldn't be coming in, and in her absence, I had a very productive morning. So productive, in fact, that I agreed to a coffee break with two of the other guys on the management team when they came to ask if I wanted to take a walk to the nearest coffee shop for a bit of fresh air.

"I've gotten so much done this week, I can hardly believe it," Isaac told us as we walked down the sunny sidewalk, our shirtsleeves rolled up in the warm late morning sun. "When Jason first suggested bringing in this time management consultant, I thought the whole thing sounded like bullshit, pardon my French, but I've got to admit, she really knows what she's talking about. I've never been so organized."

Pride shot through me before I could stop it, before I remembered that Tonia's accomplishments had absolutely nothing to do with me. Annoyance quickly replaced it as I realized that even without her around, we were still talking about her. The weekend couldn't come fast enough, when there should be no chance of anyone mentioning her at all.

"She's going to have her work cut out with me," Hal replied with a laugh. "We'll see then just how much of a miracle worker she is. Have you had any sessions with her yet, Cam?"

They both turned to look at me and I shook my head. "Not yet. I think I've got something scheduled for next week, I don't remember exactly when." I lied, of course; I knew exactly when my appointments were. Those calendar invites were burned into my brain. "She had the day off today, I guess?"

I didn't even mean to ask the question. Why did I care where she was? I really didn't.

"No, she's off with Bradyn today," Hal told me before giving Isaac a nudge. "We'll see if his plan works."

I'd missed something, apparently. "What plan?"

The two of them exchanged amused smiles as we got to the coffee shop and got in line at the counter. "He's going to try to make a move on her today," Hal explained.

"What?" The word burst out of me before I could stop it. Just how many of my colleagues were interested in my ex-girlfriend?

"Outside of work hours," Isaac elaborated, as though that made it any better. "He said he had a plan to get to know her better."

"What kind of plan?" I didn't like the sounds of that at all and I couldn't imagine why our head of human resources would be standing there laughing about it.

"Just to take her out for drinks down in Corpus Christi after they finish out at the plant," Hal explained as we got closer to the front of the counter. He leaned ahead to put in his coffee order and I had to wait until we were all finished to hear the rest of what he had to say. "He said he would try to convince her to stay overnight there, if you know what I mean. I think he's already got a hotel room booked, just in case."

Of course I knew what he meant. It would be impossible *not* to know what he meant with that shiteating grin on his face.

"And you don't have a problem with this?" I asked Isaac incredulously as we took our coffees and found a table to sit down at.

He simply shrugged. "They're adults, it's outside of work hours, and she's not technically an employee. Jason might not like it, I don't know what his position on that kind of thing is, but that's Bradyn's problem, not mine. From an HR perspective, it's all above board."

"What about from a basic human decency point of view? She's here to do a job, not get hit on." I'd gotten so worked up, I couldn't even take a drink. When I tried to pick up my take-out cup, I squeezed it so hard, the lid nearly popped right off.

"Calm down, Cam." Hal gave me a funny look. "It's not like she's your sister or something."

Did they even hear themselves? "She doesn't have to be for me to feel like it's still sleazy. She's somebody's sister."

Somebody I knew quite well, as a matter of fact, but they didn't need to know that.

"Sounds like someone else needs to get laid," Hal muttered to Isaac, gesturing towards me with his head, and I forced myself to take a deep breath. I was still new at the company and I didn't want to alienate my colleagues. Would I be laughing along with them if they were talking about anyone other than Tonia? I couldn't say for certain, and that didn't make me feel any better either. Maybe all men really were creeps.

We changed the subject and managed to dispel some of the awkwardness I'd created by the time we headed back to the office, but my uneasiness remained. Without even knowing what I hoped to find, I pulled up the company's online banking information once I returned to my desk and quickly scrolled through the accounts showing all our corporate credit cards.

Under Bradyn's card, I could see a room charge for a hotel room in Corpus Christi.

Damn it all to fucking hell.

I tried to put it out of my mind, I truly did, but by the time five o'clock came, I knew I couldn't let it go. As soon as I'd gone home and changed, I found myself getting into my truck and setting out on the three-hour drive towards a hotel in Corpus Christi I'd never been to before, without the first idea of exactly what I intended to do when I got there.

~**Tonia**~

The drive down to Corpus Christi with Bradyn took longer than I expected. He consistently went at least 10 miles an hour under the speed limit, earning him a raft of dirty looks as people sped past us on the highway, not to mention making my mind race with the mental calculations of just how much time he must waste if he always drove like that.

Several times, I had my mouth open to comment on it, but each time, I zipped it back up again. I wasn't there to give him a driving lesson. *Stay in your lane, Tonia.* My family and friends gave me that advice time and time again.

"What do you normally do while you're driving between the locations you oversee?" I asked Bradyn not long after we left Houston.

"Well, I'm new to this company, as we all are," he reminded me. "But in my last job I did a lot of travelling too. I mostly listen to music or sometimes podcasts. It's nice to have the time to unwind and think about what I need to do."

"Some downtime is important," I agreed. "And so is thinking ahead. How do you keep track of the things that you think about?"

He glanced over at me with a rather sheepish, crooked smile. "Just in my head, I guess?"

I figured as much. "You've got Bluetooth set up in here, right? Then let me show you a great program that you can dictate into."

Despite our slow speed, the rest of the trip passed quite quickly as I walked Bradyn through all the tips and tricks I had for how to make phone calls, emails, notes and more, all while staying focused on the road. By the time we pulled into the plant where he had his meetings scheduled, he looked both impressed and a little disappointed too. "I'm never going to have an excuse for just listening to my music again."

I gave him a wink. "You can always say your connection isn't working if you really need a break. I won't tell."

He grinned back at me before hopping out to come and open the truck door for me in true gentlemanly style.

Lunch awaited us when we got inside and afterwards, I accompanied Bradyn as he made a tour of the plant. However, when he went into the meetings he had planned, I excused myself to get some of my own work done, following one of my own key rules: never waste time in a meeting you don't need to be in.

After double checking all my calendar appointments for the following week, and trying not to grimace as Cam's name popped up among them far too often, I took the time to catch up with some personal emails. Dex and Shawna were inviting everyone over the following Friday evening to take a look at the new gallery space they'd purchased. My sister, Laura, two years younger than me and in her final year of her bachelor's degree, had a paper coming up for a college class that she wanted some help with, so I quickly answered her questions about that, and then I replied to Billie, our youngest sister who was in her first year of college.

I had offered a hundred times to help her set up a study schedule, but whenever she messaged me, she only wanted to talk about men.

I think I'm in love with my history TA, her latest SOS read. *Is that bad? He's not technically my professor.*

Still bad, I wrote back. *If he's in charge of your marks, steer clear. The course is only a few months long, see if he's still quite so appealing when he doesn't have any power over you anymore.*

She must have had her phone right beside her because she wrote back while I continued to scroll through my other messages. *Don't you ever just want to give into temptation, no matter what your brain says?*

I kept my reply to two simple words: *No, Billie.*

She seemed to get the message, if her string of pouting emojis in reply was any indication.

I got through the rest of my emails, including some new enquiries about my availability for the following month once my time with Barnly Oil had finished, and even after all of that, Bradyn's meeting still hadn't ended yet. With a frown, I checked my watch. It was nearly five o'clock already and we were supposed to have left to head back to Houston an hour ago. Maybe I should have gone into the meeting after all so I could keep them all on topic.

The minutes continued to tick by until the door finally opened at nearly six p.m. It would be a three-hour drive back to Houston at a normal speed; at Bradyn's speed, it would take almost four, plus we hadn't eaten anything for hours and my stomach protested at the idea of being stuck in the truck with no access to food. The granola bar I carried in my purse for emergencies wasn't going to cut it.

At least Bradyn looked apologetic as he walked over to me. "I'm so sorry that ran late, but we got a lot done. I shared some of the tips you've already given me with the guys here and they want to use them too."

I glanced over at the other men who had been in the meeting room and they all smiled and nodded in my direction, backing Bradyn up. It pleased me to hear that, but it didn't solve my more immediate problem.

Bradyn, however, had an answer for that too. "Listen, it's going to be real late by the time we get back if we head out now. I know a great Mexican place downtown and there's a nice hotel there too. We could have a relaxing evening and head back first thing in the morning if you don't have anything you need to be home for. The company'll pick up the tab, of course, since it's my fault."

That did sound a whole lot better than another four hours in the truck that evening, and I didn't have anything planned in the morning that I couldn't miss. Although I didn't have a change of clothes with me, I always carried a spare toothbrush, hairbrush, deodorant and basic makeup, just in case. You could never be too prepared.

"Sounds good to me," I agreed, and with a grin, Bradyn led the way back to his truck.

The Mexican restaurant he'd suggested turned out to be loud and bright, filled with half-drunk locals enjoying their Friday night, but the food was excellent. We chatted about food, sports and travel, typical small talk. He leaned a little too close to me at times, and I caught him looking at my chest once or twice when he thought I wasn't paying attention, but as business dinners went, I'd had worse. At least he hadn't tried to out-and-out proposition me.

Or so I thought, until we arrived at the hotel he'd suggested and he told me to take a seat on the black leather sofa in the sleek, modern lobby while he went to arrange some rooms for us. When he came back over to me, his expression had turned apologetic once again. "I'm so sorry, Tonia, but it looks like they've only got one room left."

He had to be kidding me. The cliched, tired excuse almost made me laugh, if it weren't so pathetic. "That's alright," I said, getting to my feet, and his face lit up for just a second before I finished my sentence. "We'll just go somewhere else instead. There must be hundreds of hotels in town."

"I... but... we're already here," he stuttered. "And I already took the room. Besides, you must be tired."

"I'm not tired enough to fall for something so ridiculous." Without waiting for another excuse, I marched over to the reception desk. "Excuse me, I'd like to book a room for tonight."

"Of course, ma'am," the woman behind the desk replied. "Two queens or a king?"

Exactly as I thought, and everything else about the day fell into place in my head. He didn't always drive that slow. That meeting hadn't overrun by accident. He'd planned all of this just to try to get me into bed with him, as if being in the same room was all it would take. With my eyebrows raised, I turned back to Bradyn, who had followed me over. "Fully booked, huh?"

His cheeks had turned a rather bright shade of red, the blush spreading down the back of his neck too. "Shit, I'm sorry, that was a stupid thing to do. I just think you're really beautiful and I wanted to take a shot, you know?"

"You know how you take a shot? You *ask* me if I'd like to go to dinner. You don't drive slow and stay in a meeting too long so that we have no choice but to spend the night and then try to get me into a room with you. That's creepy as hell."

"I said I'm sorry." His posture turned defensive as he got more embarrassed, but I didn't really care.

"And do you think Jason Barnly appreciates you paying for all this on his company card? Or did you at least have the good sense to pay for it yourself?"

His tight lips were all the answer I needed.

"Go on up to your room, Bradyn." I didn't have anything else to say to him. "I'll sort myself out."

He obviously had no leg left to stand on as he stormed off and I turned back to the woman at the desk, who gave me an all-too-knowing sympathetic look. "Date gone wrong?"

"Something like that." The ridiculousness of the whole situation only made me feel more tired. Why did I always seem to attract the odd ones? "Can I get the king bed, please?"

She tapped away at her screen while I pulled out my own credit card. Just as I went to hand it over to her, another voice said my name, a familiar voice but one I definitely did not expect to hear in a hotel lobby in Corpus Christi of all places.

"Tonia?"

"Cam?" What in the world would he be doing there? It made absolutely no sense and yet, there he was, rushing up to the desk beside me, relief written across his face.

"Where's Bradyn?"

"What are you doing here?"

Eventually, one of us would have to answer a question rather than just asking them, and Cam gave in first. "I came to make sure you were okay."

That might be an answer, but it didn't explain anything. "Why wouldn't I be okay? How did you know where to find me? Are you following me?"

The woman behind the desk looked between the two of us uneasily. "Seems you sure attract the weird ones, ma'am. Do you want me to call the police?"

Cam's eyes widened and for a moment, I almost felt tempted to agree just to freak him out, but in the end, I didn't want to waste anyone's time. "No, thank you. This one's harmless, for the most part."

I handed over my card so she could finish my room reservation before turning my attention back to Cam.

"Do you have a reasonable explanation for why you're here, three hours from home, at a hotel I didn't know I would be coming to until about twenty minutes ago?"

"I have an explanation," he offered weakly. "Is it reasonable? I ain't so sure about that."

I couldn't say what came over me, if I could blame it on the long day or the relief I saw in his eyes when he walked in, but something made me respond in a way neither of us expected. As I took my room key from the hotel receptionist, I pointed over to the hotel bar.

"Come on. Buy me a drink, and you can tell me all about it."

Chapter Four

~**Cam**~

Too stunned to argue, I followed Tonia into the rather upscale restaurant just off the hotel lobby. Red walls and a black ceiling with gold hanging lights wouldn't usually be my style, but I barely noticed them as we took a seat on the high stools next to the polished mahogany bar.

The place looked pretty quiet for a Friday night. Presumably, most people were still out enjoying the city or had already retired to their rooms. Besides us, only a handful of couples and a couple of people on their own sat scattered around the room, having a drink while they watched the game or scrolled through their phone. The scent of food from the tables on the other side of the room nearly made my stomach growl. The candy bars I'd scarfed down in the car couldn't really be counted as dinner.

When I pulled off the highway and into town, I realized that I had absolutely no plan for when I arrived at the hotel. Would the receptionist even tell me which room Bradyn was in? And if she did, what did I intend to do? Go and knock on the door? What on earth would I say?

I really hadn't thought things through before driving all the way down there, but as I navigated my way to the hotel I'd seen on Bradyn's credit card account, I decided that I'd go to the lobby and give Tonia a call from the hotel's phone. I had her work number on the calendar invites she'd sent me, but if I used my own phone, she might ignore it. By calling from an unknown number, I had a better chance she would answer, and then, if she needed help, I'd be right there. If she didn't, then she'd never have to know I had come all that way for nothing.

That plan quickly went out the window when I arrived and walked up to the desk to find her booking her own room and Bradyn nowhere in sight. Obviously, I'd missed something, and I was too slow on the uptake to simply hide myself and call her as I'd planned. Instead, I blurted out her name, and now I had no way to hide that I *had* followed her down there, which sounded pretty damn stalker-like when I thought about it.

I braced myself for her to go off at me when she asked if I had a reasonable explanation for my presence there, and on that occasion, I probably deserved it. But to my surprise, she didn't get upset. She actually offered to have a drink with me, and after the stress of the previous few hours, I could definitely use one. I wouldn't be heading back to Houston that night anyway. It had to be ten o'clock already, at least. I would have to get my own room at the hotel and make my way home the next morning.

The hotel would be doing a good business off of Barnly Oil that night.

"So, about this explanation you owe me, reasonable or otherwise?" Tonia prompted once we'd placed our drink orders. She'd ordered a beer, I noticed, the same as she used to. We ended up getting the same thing. "Let me have it."

I could have tried to come up with some excuse, but fatigue got the better of me. It had been a long day and an even longer week, so I simply told the truth instead. "I thought Bradyn might make a move on you tonight, and I thought you might need some backup."

Her eyebrows raised but I couldn't tell if the gesture meant she disapproved or found my statement funny. "When have I ever needed backup?"

"Never, far as I know," I admitted. "But I heard he was going to try to get you to stay here with him and it just didn't sit right with me, I guess.

Not when you're just trying to do your job. I know you *can* handle it, Tonia, I just didn't think you should have to."

"And you couldn't just phone me?" Amusement seemed to be winning out as she fished her phone out of her pocket and held it up to me, her eyebrows still higher than usual.

"I didn't think you'd answer if you saw my name," I told her honestly. "We ain't exactly been on the best of terms lately."

"Lately, as in the last six years or so?" Our drinks were set down in front of us and we both took a long sip, eager to take the edge off as we settled into the conversation.

"Pretty much, yeah. I didn't know if you'd think I was trying to mess with you, or... well, honestly, I didn't know what you might think. I just wanted to see for myself that you were alright, and if that's stupid, then I guess I'm stupid."

Might as well call myself names before she got a chance to. I knew it wouldn't be far from the tip of her tongue.

"It is kinda stupid," she agreed, with just a hint of a smile before her lips curled around the rim of the beer bottle again and she swallowed another mouthful. "You always did like being everyone's saviour."

She said something along those lines the night of Dex's wedding when she said I'd played the white knight as usual, but unlike that night, her words at the bar held no sting. She just stated them as a fact, not an accusation, and in the end, I couldn't argue with that characterization. I did like helping people out, and if she considered that some kind of crime, then I supposed I must be guilty.

In a way, that summarized the whole reason we broke up: my inability to refuse someone in need and her tendency to jump to the wildest conclusions. Those natural instincts just made us incompatible, it seemed, which was a damn shame when we were so good together in so many other ways.

"Did Bradyn actually try anything?" I wondered out loud, looking around as if he might be somewhere nearby, listening in. "Or did I really just waste my whole night for nothing?"

"Oh, you definitely wasted your night," she told me, not even bothering to hide her smile. "He made a play and I said: no, thanks. End of story. Shockingly, I know how to turn a man down all by myself."

I groaned into my beer at her teasing tone. "You're never going to let me live this down, are you?"

"Not a chance," she replied with a smirk. "I could have the whole of Sandy Creek talking about it by noon tomorrow."

"You wouldn't."

She laughed out loud, that same familiar laugh I'd heard all over the office that week. "Oh, Cam, we both know that's not true. I absolutely would."

Once again, she was absolutely right. "What's it going to cost me to keep your mouth shut? Blueberry muffins in the office every morning next week?"

Her eyes widened in surprise, the hanging lights above us reflecting in them as she stared up at me. "You remember my favourite muffin?"

I remembered a hell of a lot more than that, but I tried to shrug it off. "Some things just stick with you. Like how I can't remember what I'm meant to pick up at the store tomorrow, but I still remember which girl sat behind me in second grade."

"Jenny Palmer," we both said in unison before we both laughed.

Shoot, it felt good to laugh with her. It had been far too long.

"Muffins aren't necessary," she told me, returning to my offer. "I have a better idea. You beat me in a game of straight face, and I'll keep it a secret."

"You can't be serious."

'Straight face' was a drinking game we used to play as teenagers, sometimes in our group of friends and sometimes alone. I hadn't played it in years and Tonia had always been excellent at it, like she was at most games. It came with the territory of her being stubborn as all hell and willing to win at all costs.

"You already know you're going to lose, huh?" she teased, taking another drink. "You didn't used to be such a defeatist."

44

"I'm not being defeatist. I'm just pointing out that we're now 24 years old and in a kinda classy place and maybe we shouldn't be playing the same kind of games we used to play in my parent's basement."

An unexpected emotion flashed in her eyes at the mention of that basement, something that looked dangerously close to desire, and it sent a rush of electricity through me too. That basement had been where we made love for the first time, and the last time. I would have bet any money those memories crossed her mind at that moment, just like they did for me.

"It sounds to me like you're just afraid to lose," she said, regaining her composure and refusing to back down. "So maybe I should just text Laura right now and tell her what happened..."

As she pulled out her phone again, I reached over and placed my hand over the screen. "Alright, you win. One round; winner takes all."

Giving me a satisfied smile, she set the phone down on the bar. "You're on."

~Tonia~

I called the bartender over so I could order some shots while Cam excused himself to go to the restroom. "I just drove here from Houston," he reminded me. "If we're going to be drinking much more, I've got to pee first."

"You'll only be drinking if you lose," I reminded him, but waved my hand to tell him to go at the same time. As he walked away, I couldn't help glancing at his ass in the jeans he must have put on after work, since all week long at the office, he'd been wearing a suit. Personally, I preferred the jeans. He had definitely filled out since high school, and he hadn't been half bad then.

It was actually kind of sweet, in a completely over-the-top way, that he had come all this way just to make sure I was alright. From some guys, I would have thought they had some kind of ulterior motive, but Cam had always been that way. He'd be the guy who would give you the shirt off his back if you needed it, or the guy who would step in to be a groomsman at my brother's wedding. He could never say no if he thought someone needed help.

Did it annoy me that he thought I might not be able to handle myself with Bradyn? Maybe a little, but the prospect of being able to hold it over him more than made up for it. He'd admitted that he'd been wrong, and he knew I wouldn't let him forget it.

I'd already begun composing my first messages by the time he got back to the bar, just in time for the bartender to lay five shots out in front of each of us. The clear liquid looked deceptively innocent, the miniature glasses shining beneath the hanging light above us.

"You know the rules," I told him, pretty sure that he still would even though it had been years since we'd done this. "Whatever I text you, you have to read out with a straight face. Any laugh, any wince, any kind of face at all, and you have to drink."

"I remember." The stillness of his voice contrasting with the intensity of those deep brown eyes was enough to send me straight back to the basement he'd referenced earlier, to my first kiss and so many other firsts we'd shared there together. Butterflies fluttered in my stomach at the memory, the way they used to at the sight of him.

Those days were long gone, though, and that train of thought wouldn't help me to keep my composure. I had to focus on the game. "Do you want to go first, or me?"

"You send me one first," he decided. I'd only added his phone number to my phone earlier this week, when I added everyone at Barnly Oil's numbers, and at the time, I certainly never expected to be using it while sitting across from him in a bar in Corpus Christi. Life sure took some funny turns sometimes.

I quickly reviewed the messages I'd already started typing and chose one I thought would be a good place to start. Like a hawk, I watched his face as he opened it and read it over, looking for any twitch of his lips, any wrinkling of his nose, anything I could pounce on to prove that he had failed at the task.

To my disappointment, he read it with a completely straight face, first to himself and then out loud: "Tonia Callahan is the world's best driver. I feel completely safe and relaxed when I'm in the car with her."

Damn it. He used to hate my driving so I thought that might get to him. The old Cam wouldn't have been able to say that with a straight face. This might be a little harder than I thought.

As if to prove my point, he raised his eyebrows at me as he lowered the phone. "Really, Sugar? That's the best you've got?"

"Shut up and take your turn."

He must have already been thinking about it in the restroom because he typed something in without hesitation, and a second later, the message flashed up on my phone.

Forcing myself to keep my expression completely neutral, I looked up at him as I spoke the words out loud. "It doesn't bother me at all when words get spelled wrong in advertisements."

Cam cracked a smile even if I didn't. "Alright, your lying skills have improved. Looks like we need to turn this up a notch."

"Agreed." I sent the next message in my list over to him, and I could have sworn the muscles in his cheek twitched even if his lips didn't move.

"I keep a cheerleading outfit in my closet that I put on for special occasions. It makes my ass look great and the ladies love it."

Seriously? Not even a wobble. Who was this stone-faced man and what had he done with Cameron Bailey?

"That's how you want to play this?" His smile came as he typed something else into his phone and when I read it, I bit hard on the inside of my cheek to keep from reacting.

My eyes raised to his, only to find him watching me with a smug smirk. "Come on, Sugar. Out loud."

He'd asked for it now. Clearing my throat, I read it out in as flat a tone as I could manage. "My first boyfriend ruined all other men for me. No one will ever satisfy me like he did."

As I reached the end, still completely straight-faced, I could have sworn disappointment flashed in his eyes.

"Bad move, Bailey," I told him now that I had passed his test. "You just put sex on the table."

"I didn't say anything specifically about sex," he tried to argue, but his protest came too late. The damage had already been done.

When he got my next message, he only made it half-way through. "I have a hard time concentrating at work because all I can think about is Jason Barnly bending me over his desk and..." He couldn't even finish, choosing to take the shot rather than complete the sentence. His cheeks hollowed at the alcohol's bitter sting, and he gave his head a shake as he swallowed it down. "You're going to regret that, Sugar."

"Try me."

We went back and forth, the things we were texting each other getting progressively filthier and more absurd at the same time, until we each only had one shot left and the room had grown distinctly blurrier than it had been when we started.

"Your turn," Cam said, squinting down at his phone as he tried to type something out. Just watching him made me laugh, and therein lay the danger of the game. The drunker you got, the harder it became to keep a straight face. "There you go."

My phone buzzed and I opened my text message, the words dancing around the screen as I tried to focus on them. "If they made a Cam-shaped disco, I would buy one for every day of the week." Confused, I looked up at him. "What?"

"That's not what it says," he protested, taking my phone from me clumsily. He brought it right up to his face to read it and then swore when he realized I had, in fact, said it correctly. "It was supposed to say dildo. Fucking auto-correct."

That set me giggling, which set him off too. "Too bad for you," I taunted. "Now, it's your turn."

I knew I had to pull out the big guns here so I wrote the most ridiculous thing I could think of, a line from one of Cam's favourite movies that he always used to say for me in a ridiculous dolphin voice whenever he wanted to make me smile, and when he opened up the text, he started laughing before he even got one word out.

"Yes! Victory!" My celebration got the attention of just about everyone else in the bar, which had started to fill up more as the evening wore on, and Cam quickly shushed me.

"Keep it between us, Sugar. These folks don't need to know all the details, but I suppose you're right. You won fair and square."

He picked up his last shot, but I grabbed it from his hands and drank it myself as he watched me in surprise. Somehow, we were suddenly very close to each other.

"What'd you do that for?"

"I didn't play fair," I had to admit. "That line always makes you laugh. It feels like a cheat."

"*You* always make me laugh." His eyes were warm, and far too close to me, and before I even knew what happened, his lips were on mine.

It all felt incredibly familiar and yet completely new at the same time. His kiss was firmer and more assured than it used to be, but he still tasted the same, other than the shots we'd just drank. His scent filled my nose and his hand cupped the side of my face, just like always, holding me like I was the most precious thing in the world.

I couldn't say how long it lasted, but probably no more than a few seconds before we both came to our senses and pulled apart.

"Sorry, that was..."

"No, I know, I didn't mean..."

"... too many shots..."

"... long day..."

We both mumbled excuses until Cam asked the bartender for the bill and gave me a sheepish smile. "Think we better call it a night."

We definitely should. Cam typed something into his phone while I checked mine for the time, and I'd just made it out as 11:42 when another message popped up on the screen.

"I thought we were done," I reminded him, smiling again as I opened it and began to read out loud. "Had to take Shawna to the hospital today. Just got the results and the cancer is back."

It took a moment for the words to make sense to me, to realize that they weren't from Cam at all but from my brother, Dex, and when I looked up at Cam in surprise and dismay, he looked just as concerned as I felt.

"Are you serious?"

I could only nod as I looked down at the phone, rereading the message to make sure I hadn't imagined it. Both my good mood and the awkwardness of that unexpected kiss completely evaporated, as though I'd been dunked into ice water. "I've got to go there. I have to get back."

I knew the mere idea was ridiculous; we were three hours away and neither of us were in any state to drive, but that didn't matter, not compared to my family needing me.

"I'll get a taxi," Cam promised. "Hang tight, I'll be right back."

He went off to the reception desk while I tapped out a reply to my brother, reading it four times to make sure I hadn't messed it up in my drunken state. I only managed four words, but I knew what they'd mean to him and I didn't want to get it wrong.

I'm on my way.

~Cam~

Although it only took about ten minutes for the taxi to arrive, it felt like forever. Tonia had nothing with her but her purse and her business bag, since she hadn't been planning to stay overnight here in the first place, and as we stood side-by-side outside the front door of the hotel, waiting for the car to pull up, I didn't know what to do.

In another life, I would have offered to take her bags for her. I would have put my arms around her and comforted her, encouraging her to share what she felt, but that wasn't our relationship anymore and it hadn't been for a long time.

She didn't want me to see her vulnerability, and I didn't want to see it either, because then I would have to remember that beneath the tough exterior and the look of disdain she usually threw in my direction these days, the girl I once loved still lurked. The girl I would have done anything for, including driving three hours for no reason and taking a taxi back the same distance that same night, even though I would have to come right back tomorrow to pick up my truck.

I definitely didn't want to do anything foolish like that.

I'd asked for an SUV rather than a sedan when I called for a taxi, and once we settled ourselves inside, I told Tonia to take a nap.

"How can I sleep?" she asked, sounding dangerously close to tears. "I can't believe they have to go through this again."

"It's not fair," I quickly agreed. "But you'll be a lot more use to Dex if you're rested and a little more sober. Besides, you know you'll be out like a light as soon as we hit the highway anyway."

More memories flashed across my mind: driving along quiet back roads in my old truck, Tonia's head resting on my shoulder as I drove us both home in the dark after a night out somewhere. If she drove, she could stay awake no problem, but as a passenger in a car at night, she would be asleep within minutes. It took a little longer that night, the emotional strain obviously taking its toll on her, but eventually, the motion of the car, the darkness, and the lingering effects of the alcohol all combined and her eyes began to drift closed.

When her head fell onto my shoulder, I left it there. She needed the rest, I told myself.

Only when we got back to Houston and the taxi stopped at a traffic light did she lift her head again, looking around in confusion for a moment before it all came back to her: where we were and why.

"Oh." She looked down at my shoulder in dismay as she realized where she'd been sleeping. "Sorry. You should have pushed me off."

"It's no big deal, Sugar."

Though I said that, as soon as she turned to look out the window, I stretched out my aching muscles that I hadn't been able to move for the last few hours, biting my tongue to keep from groaning in relief.

"Are we almost there?"

She turned back to me and I quickly froze in place so she wouldn't notice me stretching. "Just a few more minutes. You've had a few texts on your phone."

I gestured to her purse that had fallen onto the floor and she quickly picked it up and pulled her phone out, scrolling through and responding to the important ones as the taxi pulled up outside the hospital.

"Go on ahead, I got this," I told her. Still staring at her phone, she headed through the doors while I settled up with the taxi driver. By the time I got inside, I couldn't see Tonia or any of the Callahan crew so I went to the reception desk. Though the shots had mostly worn off during the long drive, the lights still felt too bright, everything a little too white. "Howdy. I'm looking for Shawna Armstrong. Cancer ward, I guess."

The woman at the desk typed into her computer for a moment before shaking her head. "No one by that name here."

For a moment, I had a stupid, not-totally-sober hope that maybe somehow this had all been a mistake. Maybe Shawna hadn't really had a relapse and it had been some kind of stupid prank; not that it would be funny, but a joke would be better than the alternative.

When I thought about it a second longer, though, I realized my mistake. "Sorry, it's probably under Callahan. Shawna Callahan."

That did the trick and I was given directions to the waiting room where Tonia had found her parents, her sisters, and Dex, who appeared to be giving Tonia an update. He was the first to see me when I walked in, his eyes widening in surprise as he recognized me. "Cam? What are you doing here?"

Tonia answered before I had a chance to. "I didn't get a chance to tell you that Cam helped me get back from Corpus Christi. It's... kind of a long story."

"It would have to be." Dex shook his head in bewilderment before returning to the matter at hand. "Anyway, I'm just about to send everyone home anyway. Shawna's family's already been and gone, we were just waiting for you, Tonia, but now that you're here, ain't nothing else anyone can do tonight. Shawna's already asleep so go on and go to bed yourselves, and you can come back tomorrow and see her then."

"What about you, Dex?" Tonia put her hand on her brother's arm, looking up at him in concern. "You need some sleep too."

"There's a chair in her room." When the others began to protest, he quickly silenced them all. "Y'all know you're not going to change my mind, so just go. If you need something to worry about, find out what Tonia was doing in Corpus Christi with the devil himself over there. No offense, Cam."

"Your wife's sick so I'm going to let that one go for now, but I'm keeping score, Dex."

He gave me a grateful smile, appreciating that I tried to keep things light for everyone's benefit and he headed back towards the patient rooms while everyone else gathered up their things to leave.

"Where are y'all staying tonight?" Tonia asked her parents and sisters

"I guess we've got to find ourselves a hotel," her mama replied. "Doesn't have to be fancy, just a bed will do."

"You can come stay with me," Tonia offered, and when they shot her an incredulous look, she added a qualifier. "Well, not all of you, but some of you, at least."

Her parents exchanged looks. "Maybe Laura and Billie can stay with you," Mr Callahan suggested. "And we'll find a place just for us."

"I've got room."

The words came out of my mouth before I had a chance to think them through and everyone turned to look at me in surprise, as though they'd forgotten I was still there.

The words kept pouring out beneath the weight of their stares. "I mean, if you just need a bed for the night, I've got the space. No point in you spending the money on a hotel if you don't have to."

Tonia's parents looked at each other again, having a whole conversation with their eyes before Mrs Callahan gave me a smile. "That's very kind of you, Cam. If you're sure it won't be a bother..."

"Not at all. Happy to help."

We all headed back to the hospital entrance and the line of taxis outside. Tonia and her sisters took the first one to head to her place and Tonia gave me a small smile before she got in. "Thanks for ... well, everything, Cam."

I tried to shrug it off. "It was the least I could do."

That made her laugh, her face brightening with that beautiful smile of hers as she called me on my bullshit, just like always. "Absolutely nothing about tonight was the least you could do. And now you've got to go back down there tomorrow and get your truck, don't you?"

I shrugged again. What could I say? She knew I did.

"It's a terrible waste of time," she told me, slipping into her work voice that I recognized from the office. "You need to learn to be far more efficient."

"I'm sure you'll teach me what I need to know, Sugar."

"I'll try."

She gave me another smile and for a moment, we both just stood there, simply looking at each other. All I could think of was the way it had felt back in the bar earlier when I kissed her. Or when she kissed me, I couldn't quite say which way it went.

And damn it all if I didn't want to do it again.

But this wasn't the time or the place, not at the hospital with her whole family watching, so I took a step back and she gave me a nod and got in the car, while I headed to the next taxi with her parents, making polite conversation with them on the way back to my apartment.

It hadn't been at all the evening I expected, but life had always been a whirlwind whenever Tonia was around. Even after all these years, that definitely hadn't changed.

Chapter Five

~**Tonia**~

"So?" My sisters both cornered me as soon as we walked into my clean and modern one-bedroom apartment, and Laura took the lead on questioning. "What's going on with you and Cam?"

"Nothing is going on," I tried to deflect, stepping out of my high-heeled shoes with a sigh of relief. When I put them on that morning, I never imagined I'd be wearing them so long, and the hardwood floor of my hallway had never felt so good on my bare feet. "Laura, you can sleep with me and Billie gets the couch."

My distraction worked on my youngest sister, at least, as she looked into the living room in dismay. The two-seater couch sat at a right angle to a matching armchair, both facing the wall-mounted TV. "Why do I have to sleep on the couch? It's too short."

"And you're the shortest one of us," I pointed out. "That's why it has to be you."

"You're not getting off the hook that easily," Laura protested as I walked into my bedroom with the two of them in close pursuit, stuck to me like shadows. "Last time you saw Cam, you said you'd rather be locked in a room full of angry yellowjackets rather than spend another evening with him."

Had I said that? I didn't recall using those exact words, but to be fair, it sounded like something I would say. Thinking back over the evening as I pulled out my earrings and took off my necklace and watch, placing everything in its proper place so I wouldn't have to waste time looking for them the next time I wanted them, I had to admit that might have been an exaggeration.

"I didn't spend the evening with him on purpose. It just kind of turned out that way, and it was... okay."

It had been more than okay, actually, in a rather confusing way. We had fun at the bar before that kiss came out of nowhere. His quiet support once I got Dex's text had actually been really sweet. At any time, he could have washed his hands of the whole evening and left me to handle it on my own. It didn't affect him personally in any way, and yet, he never hesitated. In his usual calm, steady way, he'd been there for me, just like he used to be.

In the end, I couldn't put a label on the night as a whole.

"That look he gave you by the taxi suggested a lot more than 'okay'," Laura pointed out, and Billie nodded enthusiastically.

"I don't know if I've ever seen anyone smoulder before, but that look *smouldered*."

"Why are we talking about this?" I tried as I pulled two extra pairs of pajamas out of my drawer and threw them at my sisters. "We should be focused on Dex and Shawna."

"We're not talking about them because that whole situation is depressing as hell," Laura countered. "And besides, we hardly ever get to see you flustered. This is kind of fun."

"I'm not flustered," I protested. "I'm drunk. There's a difference."

She rolled her eyes at me while I grabbed my own pajamas and started to get undressed.

"I never understood exactly why you guys broke up in the first place," Billie complained. "No one will ever tell me the whole story. Every time I ask, everyone just says 'it's in the past'."

Billie had only been twelve years old when things ended between me and Cam, so I hadn't exactly opened up to her about it at the time. However, Laura and I had both been making a concerted effort to treat her more like an adult since she technically became one, rather than continuing to treat her as just our baby sister, so although I didn't really want to rehash it all, I decided to give in anyway.

Laura had a point, after all: revisiting my past drama would be better than worrying about Shawna when we couldn't do a damn thing about her health.

"Go get ready for bed and I'll tell you all about it."

Billie squealed in excitement as she made a beeline for the bathroom. Once we'd each taken a turn, we gathered back on my queen-sized bed, the most expensive piece of furniture in my one-bedroom apartment. A good night's sleep was key to productivity; I told my clients that and I firmly believed it. My mattress might have cost me a month's salary, but I never regretted it.

"Stop me if I tell you anything you already know," I instructed Billie before settling into the story. "Cam and I started dating officially when we were fifteen but we had known each other since forever. We did everything together. You must remember how much time he spent at our house."

Billie nodded so enthusiastically that the bed bounced beneath her. "I remember when Jill Mason moved to town, she thought Cam must be my brother because every time she came over to see me, he'd be there."

That sounded about right. "Well, I was completely in love with him. I never even looked at anyone else, even though there were plenty of other guys who were interested."

"Sure there were," Laura interjected sarcastically before giving Billie a nudge. "If you listen to her, she'll have you thinking the whole football team were lining up for her."

"Maybe not the *whole* team, but at least the offensive line," I shot back, making her grin. "Why wouldn't they be? Homecoming queen, class president, and a shoo-in for prom queen."

My voice caught on the last words, to my great annoyance. *No way* would I let myself get emotional over that, not after six years. I had gotten over it, just like I had gotten over Cam, and no one could convince me otherwise.

"I remember how cool you were," Billie assured me even as Laura rolled her eyes. "All my friends wanted to be you."

As flattering as that might be, no one would have wanted to be me by the end of the story. "Prom was a huge deal, as you could guess. It always is. We were having ours just before graduation, and I had my dress picked out for months. It would be our last big event before leaving high school behind, and everyone knew Cam and I would go together. We hadn't gone to a single thing with anyone else ever since our first day of freshman year."

"Spoiler alert," Laura stage-whispered, leaning over to Billie. "They didn't end up going together."

"I remember that too," Billie assured us. "What I don't really know is why."

My lips tightened as the memories flashed back through my mind, that same pit opening in the bottom of my stomach that always appeared when I thought back to that time in my life. "Well, a few weeks before prom, Cam started acting differently. He'd tell me he had things to do but wouldn't tell me what they were. He wouldn't answer his phone when I called. At first, I thought maybe he was planning some kind of surprise for me, 'cause honestly, it wouldn't be out of character for him to go all out."

I could still remember how I tried to push all my doubts aside, telling myself I was getting worked up over nothing. Cam loved me; he told me so, and he proved it in almost everything he did. He wouldn't do anything to hurt me.

Or so I thought.

"The first inkling I had about the real story was when Kara Beckett cornered me in the locker room after volleyball practice one day. Do you remember Kara?"

"I know her younger sister, Raenne," Billie told me. "I think they inherited the same bitch gene."

Her bluntness made me smile, and she had it exactly right. "That's them. She came up to me, acting all innocent and asking me why I never mentioned that Cam had become such good friends with Marley Stevens. Though I knew she wanted to wind me up, I also knew she always had her ear to the ground for gossip, so I couldn't help asking her what she meant. She told me that Cam had been over at Marley's house almost every night for the last week. Not just in the evening either, but staying overnight. Kara said she saw him leaving one morning, wearing the same clothes he'd worn at school the day before."

"No!" Billie's eyes went wide, and in her expression, I could almost see my own shocked disbelief when Kara told me about it too. "What about her parents?"

"I asked that too. She said they'd been out of town for a while and Marley had been staying there on her own."

Billie chewed on her lip, searching her memory. "I don't really remember Marley. Was she a friend of yours?"

I shook my head as I glanced over to the big window in my room that overlooked the Houston skyline. Most of the lights in the surrounding skyscrapers were off since most normal people would be asleep in the middle of the night. Sometimes, looking out that window, I almost imagined I could see the little town where I grew up if I just squinted hard enough. "I only knew Marley in passing. She was a year younger than us and kept to herself a lot. People found her a bit strange, so even though she was pretty, she didn't have a lot of friends. I didn't think Cam really knew her either, until Kara told me he did."

"Maybe it wasn't what it looked like?" Billie suggested, and I shot her a disapproving look.

"You don't think that didn't cross my mind? I asked Cam flat out the next time I saw him if he knew Marley, and he said 'not really'. He definitely didn't say anything about spending time with her."

The way my stomach sank at his response still lingered in my memory. If I closed my eyes, I could almost feel it again. Kara might have been exaggerating, but her stories usually had some basis in truth. If there was nothing going on between them that he had to be guilty about, why would he lie to me?

"You know me," I continued, giving Billie a shrug. "I had to keep digging, so that night, I went over to Marley's house myself. I hid across the street and I saw Cam show up. He certainly acted like someone who had something to hide. When he got to her house, he looked around, making sure no one could see him before he turned up the path and went to her door."

Billie had leaned so far forward, she'd almost folded herself in half. "What did you do? Did you go and knock?"

"I would have, but before I could, I saw a light come on over on the other side of the house. The curtains were open, so I decided to just go take a quick peek."

"You spied on them through the window?" Billie wrinkled her nose and she and Laura both laughed. "You're a freak."

"I'm *thorough*," I argued. "They could say whatever they wanted when they answered the door, but if I saw it for myself, I would know for sure. Maybe he'd be helping her with her math homework, or maybe they'd just be watching TV. It wouldn't explain why he lied to me, but at least I could trust my eyes."

In my mind, I could still feel my heart pounding as I snuck up to the house, trying to avoid being seen as I crept closer to the window. Dozens of potential scenarios flashed across my imagination, a variety of innocent things they might be up to and how I could laugh at myself afterwards about how paranoid I'd been. I would tell Cam and he would laugh too, and soon, it would be just one more funny story we had to share. I convinced myself of it.

Once again, I was proven wrong.

"What did you see?" Billie asked breathlessly.

"They were in her bedroom. He sat on her bed while she paced back and forth, ranting about something, waving her arms around. The more upset she got, the farther he leaned forward, until he got up and wrapped his arms around her, hugging her really tightly just like he always did with me. She hugged him back, putting her arms around him like they'd done it a hundred times before."

Though it had happened years earlier, my heart pounded as I relived it all: the disbelief, the hurt, and the anger I'd felt, seeing her in his embrace.

"Did they kiss?" Billie asked softly.

"I don't know. I didn't stick around to find out. Before they could see me, I took off back home. When I got there, I texted him, pretending not to know anything, just asking how his night had been and how things were going, and he never wrote me back. I didn't sleep a wink all night, and by the time the morning came, I was *pissed off*."

Billie and Laura both nodded in understanding. They wouldn't have expected anything different.

"I went to school ready to confront him, and who did I see as soon as I walked in? Kara freaking Beckett, who was only too happy to tell me that the news was all over school that Cam and Marley were going to prom together."

Billie gasped, and even though Laura already knew the whole story, she still winced too.

"You must have let him have it," Billie guessed, knowing me as well as she did. "I can't imagine you took that lying down."

"Of course I didn't," I confirmed. "I marched straight up to him, right there in the hallway in front of everyone, and asked him why the hell I had to find out from someone else that he had another date to the prom."

"Did he deny it?" Billie asked.

I shook my head again. "No. He simply said he had planned to tell me later, that he would explain it all to me, whatever the hell *that* was supposed to mean. I told him he didn't have to explain a thing, that despite what he seemed to think, he hadn't completely fooled me, and I told him about seeing him at Marley's the night before. *He* had the nerve to get mad at *me* for spying on him, and we both shouted at each other until we got sent to the principal's office. By that point, I couldn't hold back, and I ended up swearing at both Cam *and* the principal, which got me sent home for the day and banned from attending the prom, which was hardly a problem anyway since I no longer had a date."

The anger that had boiled over that day still simmered inside me if I gave it the slightest bit of attention, and I took a deep breath to calm myself once I got the whole story out.

"Anyway, that was it, really. Cam never apologized. He even tried to claim that *I* owed *him* an apology for not giving him a chance to explain. He really did take Marley to the prom, and our relationship ended. We've never spent a full evening in each other's company again, at least not until last night."

Billie had a few more questions, which I answered for her before insisting that we all go to bed before the morning came, which would be in a matter of a few hours by that point. As I lay in my bed in the dark, listening to Laura's quiet snores beside me, I actually felt grateful that Billie had brought the whole thing up.

I needed the reminder of just how much Cam hurt me and just how betrayed I felt by what he'd done, so that what happened in the bar that night didn't happen again. Cam belonged to my past, and aside from having to work together for a few weeks, he would remain there. I had a very good reason for keeping my distance, and I needed to keep that in mind, no matter how much I might be tempted to forget it.

A MATTER OF TIME

~Cam~

In the morning, I made a quick breakfast for the Callahans before calling a taxi for them and sending them back to the hospital. I could tell Mrs Callahan wanted to offer me something in return for letting them stay, but her usual go-to thank-you gesture would be to invite the person she wanted to thank over for dinner. That didn't really work in this situation; first, because I lived in Houston while they were still in Sandy Creek, and second, because things were still awkward and unsettled between me and Tonia. I insisted that I didn't need any kind of reward and I asked them to tell Dex and Shawna I'd be praying for them.

Since I let the Callahans sleep in my bed while I took the pull-out couch, my back felt a little stiff that morning and the prospect of sitting on a bus for a few hours really didn't appeal to me. However, it would be a lot cheaper than another taxi ride like the one we took last night when I ended up having to pay the driver for his time to go back to Corpus Christi too. It probably would have been cheaper to buy a used car for the night and ditch it in the morning.

The money didn't bother me too much though. I made decent money and I could afford to take the hit. Not that I splashed my money around without good reason; I grew up on the poorer side of the middle-class line and I knew what it felt like to go without, but I also didn't see the point of having money sitting around in the bank when you could use it to help someone out. I didn't begrudge spending some of it to help Tonia out when she needed it.

It also explained how I ended up getting to know Marley Stevens in the first place, and how I learned that trying to help someone out wasn't always as straightforward as it seemed. Sometimes, it led to a whole hell of a lot of unintended consequences.

It was almost eleven o'clock by the time I arrived back at the hotel in Corpus Christi where I'd parked my truck the night before. Trying to be inconspicuous, I ducked into the hotel lobby to use the restroom before I began the long drive back to Houston, and when I came back out, a familiar figure stood at the check-out desk, just a few feet away from me.

Putting my head down, I tried to walk past without being seen, but luck didn't seem to be on my side.

"Cam?" Bradyn sounded understandably surprised to see me as he gave me a curious smile. "What the heck are you doing here?"

Well, crap. What could I say? Explaining it to Tonia had been bad enough, but at least I'd been on her side. When it came to Bradyn, I'd actually come down to thwart him in the first place, and now, I was getting called out on it. It almost made me want to stop trying to do nice things for anyone when it kept blowing up in my face.

I tried to play it casual and avoid his question as I went over to shake his hand. "Oh, hey, Bradyn. What brings you to town?"

"I'm here for work," he explained, still looking confused about my presence. "I had a meeting that ran long and stayed over. What about you?"

"Oh, just... uh, came down to see a baseball game." I blurted out the first thought that came into my head, though I had no idea if the local team even had a game that day.

Bradyn's face lit up as he leaned against the desk, oblivious to anyone else who might need to speak to the receptionist. "I didn't know you were a fan. I've got season tickets to the Astros but I've never been to see the Hooks."

The Corpus Christi Hooks were the local minor league team and one of the farm teams for the Houston Astros. Luckily, my dad was a huge fan and I'd spend enough time chatting with him to be able to talk somewhat knowledgeably on the subject. "It's interesting to see what kind of talent they've got down here sometimes. Makes a nice day out."

He glanced outside at the bright blue sky, the perfect setting for an afternoon game. "Shoot, I'd love to go with you, but I've got to take Tonia back to the city. I'm just waiting to hear from her."

He thought Tonia was still there? With everything else going on, she must not have had a chance to tell him she'd already left, and if she'd gone back to the hospital, chances were she had her phone off. If he waited for a reply from her, he might be waiting a long time.

"Tonia Callahan, you mean?" I asked, pretending that I had to struggle to remember her name. "The consultant from work?"

He nodded in agreement. "She came down with me yesterday so I'm her ride."

Quickly, I put everything together in my head, trying to come up with a plan to cover Tonia and spare Bradyn the embarrassment of realizing he'd been completely forgotten about. "Would you give me just a second, Bradyn? I just remembered there's a call I need to make."

After he nodded again, I stepped back into the restaurant where we sat the night before and quickly sent Tonia a text: *If you get something from Bradyn, don't respond to it. I've taken care of it.*

Next, I called the hotel reception desk. From where I stood, I could see the receptionist as she picked up my call. "Good morning. I've got a message for Bradyn Mclaren from Tonia Callahan."

I explained how she'd had a family emergency and had to leave, and when the receptionist assured me she'd pass the message on, I checked the website for the Corpus Christi Hooks and found that there was, in fact, a home game this afternoon. Finally, something seemed to be going my way. I bought a single ticket out in left field with lots of empty seats around it before heading back into the lobby to where Bradyn had taken a seat on one of the couches.

I sat down next to him, flashing him a casual smile. "Sorry about that. You know, I was just thinking: it seems odd that Tonia's not getting back to you. Isn't her whole deal being super-organized?"

That made him laugh. "Exactly. I didn't peg her for a late sleeper."

"Maybe she left some kind of message for you at the desk?" I suggested as innocently as possible and, sure enough, when he went to check, he found a message waiting.

"Good call," he told me gratefully when he came back. "She's already gone and I'd've been sitting here waiting forever. I guess I'm not in any hurry to get back to the city now so if you don't mind some company for the game today..."

"That'd be great," I quickly agreed. "I'm sure we can pick up an extra ticket at the field."

That was how I ended up spending the day with the guy who had tried to hit on Tonia the night before. He ended up confessing the whole thing to me as we sat on our plastic outfield seats together under the warm Texas sun, eating hot dogs and drinking beer.

"I thought it would be kind of charming," he told me as he took a swig from his bottle. "But she said it came across creepy, and looking back, I kind of see her point."

I couldn't argue with that, but the more we talked, the more I could see he wasn't such a bad guy, really. He did something stupid, but hadn't we all? After the blunt refusal he got from Tonia, he'd never try that particular trick again.

"Women are confusing," he complained good-naturedly. "They like all that shit in a romance novel, but if you do it in real life, you're a freak."

"It's a mystery," I agreed, trying not to laugh. "Don't ask me for advice though, I don't have a clue either. I'm still waiting for the magic formula."

Tonia did text me back during the game in response to my message, but her answer contained only one word: *Okay.*

No thanks, no update on how things were going at the hospital, and definitely no joking around. She couldn't make it any clearer that whatever ceasefire we'd had in place the night before had been lifted, so by the time I finally got home that evening, I was pretty much resigned to the fact that I would have to go into the week ahead expecting the worst.

~Tonia~

By Monday morning, things were as back to normal as they could be. Shawna and Dex had a new treatment plan that would involve her staying in the hospital for a few days to start another round of chemotherapy but she should be going home by the middle of the week, and they were still determined to have us all over on Friday to show off the new gallery space. We tried to tell them it could wait, but Shawna insisted she needed something fun to look forward to. I offered to help organize food and drinks for everyone, and Dex gratefully accepted.

With all that in place, I returned for another week at Barnly Oil that would hopefully be a little less eventful than the last one.

I had my phone off on Saturday when Bradyn texted to let me know he was ready to go. I had completely forgotten about letting him know I'd left, but by the time I saw his message, Cam had already messaged me to say he'd taken care of it. I didn't know what that meant, but I didn't want to encourage any further conversation by asking; my talk with my sisters had reminded me exactly why Cam and I weren't friends, and I had no reason to act like we were.

Bradyn texted me again on Sunday, that time to apologize for his behaviour on Friday and I told him not to worry about it so long as he didn't try anything like that again. He assured me he wouldn't, so as I headed into the office in another trendy suit Laura had selected for me and gave Marianne a smile of greeting, everything seemed back under control.

"Have you got a minute, Tonia?" Jason headed me off before I could head to my first meeting of the day. My morning would be spent doing my initial session with Cam and the afternoon with a man named Jeremy who looked after the business' supply chain.

"Of course," I agreed with a smile. Early as usual, I could spare a minute. "What's up?"

He led me into his office, letting me take a seat first while he closed the door behind us. Once he'd settled behind his desk, he explained why he'd invited me in. "I heard you got delayed in Corpus Christi on Friday."

News sure travelled fast in the company; I definitely couldn't complain about the efficiency of the gossip. "What exactly did you hear?" I wondered out loud. Had Bradyn confessed to him as well as apologizing to me? Or did Cam say something?

"Just that your meeting ran long and you had to stay overnight. You can charge your room to the company, and I just wanted to apologize. I know your time's valuable, and we don't take it for granted."

"I thought that was my line," I teased him and he grinned back at me, looking relieved that I had no hard feelings about it. "If you already know the value of time, what do you need me for?"

"I hear you're doing a great job," he praised me, which made me smile in return. "I'm free for lunch today if you have time to catch up. I'd love to hear what you've identified as our problem areas so far."

"That sounds great."

As we made plans for lunch, I remembered Dex's question about whether Jason's interest in me extended outside the realm of business, but I didn't really get any of those signals from him. It sounded like a business meeting and nothing more.

After confirming the details, I left Jason and made my way over to Cam's office. He had already settled behind his desk, wearing a blue-and-white striped shirt that had no business looking as good on him as it did. His eyes were on his computer screen, and when he saw me, he quickly clicked a few things closed.

Not suspicious at all. Looked like he still didn't want me to know exactly what he was up to.

"Morning. I almost thought you were gonna be late." He offered me a smile but I thought I detected a hesitation behind it. Was he actually... *nervous?* I had never associated that word with Cameron Bailey.

"I just had to talk to Jason for a minute," I explained as I walked in. "Do you want the door closed or open?"

He glanced towards the open doorway as if it were a lifeline from the horror of being in an enclosed space with me. "Open, I guess. How're Dex and Shawna doing?"

"As good as can be expected." I had no intention of sharing more than that with him. Setting my bag down on his desk, I grabbed the chair in front of me and pulled it around to the same side he was sitting on so I could see his screen. "We're here to get you organized, though, so let's dive right in."

He swallowed as I took a seat next to him, and I wondered if the scent of my perfume affected him just as much as his cologne did for me. It seemed that way, but unlike him, I had no intention of letting it show.

"I... uh, I thought you might like some coffee first. You know, Monday morning and all. Here." From the top of the small filing cabinet next to him, he grabbed a take-out coffee cup and a small brown paper bag.

As nice as the gesture might be, I didn't want to set that kind of tone for the week. "Look, Cam, I know Friday was strange and confusing. At least, that's how it felt for me. But now that we're in the office, you need to treat me the same as you would any other consultant. Would you buy coffee and a blueberry muffin for someone here to audit your taxes?"

He hadn't told me he had a blueberry muffin in the bag, but after he brought it up the other day, I made an educated guess and he didn't deny it.

"Actually, I would," he told me with a shrug, seeming to relax a little more after I made my expectations clear. "This is me, Tonia. You don't have to drink the coffee, but that ain't gonna stop me from buying it."

If that didn't sum Cam up perfectly, I really didn't know what would.

"Well, it would be a shame to let it go to waste," I gave in, taking it from him. The coffee did smell very good, and just the idea of the warm muffin had my mouth watering. "But only because it's Monday."

"Got it," he promised. "So, where do we start?"

As soon as we got into my planned outline for the morning, the time actually passed quickly. He was already doing a lot of things right, and I recognized a lot of his organizational tactics from things he used to do even back in high school. When he told me about exactly what his job entailed, I could hear the enthusiasm he had for it, and in spite of everything, I found myself feeling pleased for him that he enjoyed his job, just like I did.

Almost before I knew it, my phone gently chimed to let me know our time was up.

"That should give you some things to get started on, at least," I told him as I packed my things away. The coffee and muffin had long since disappeared, but I brushed a few lingering crumbs into the trash. "We're together again tomorrow afternoon, so you can let me know if you have questions then."

He gave me a rather impressed smile. "I enjoyed that, Sugar. You know your stuff."

"Tonia," I reminded him, glancing quickly over at the door to make sure no one had heard that before returning the compliment. "You know what you're talking about too."

"I better if I want to keep my job," he replied with a laugh.

"Well, I can put in a good word for you with the boss," I teased him back. "We're just about to go for lunch to review how things are going."

The smile immediately dropped from Cam's face. "You and Jason are going for lunch? Again?"

"Is that a problem?" I paused in the middle of packing my things back into my bag. "It's not really any of your business."

"It's not," he quickly agreed, glancing at the door as well to make sure we were still alone. Maybe we should have closed it after all. "It's just that after what happened on Friday with Bradyn, I just don't want you to end up in another awkward situation. Jason... well, I think he likes you."

"He told you that?" Maybe Dex had been onto something after all, and I had to admit to feeling flattered at the idea. But why would Jason have been talking to Cam about me? "I didn't think you had said anything to anyone here about knowing me."

"I haven't," he assured me. "And he didn't tell me, exactly, but I got that vibe. Look, I ain't trying to tell you what to do, Tonia. Trust me, I know how well that works. I just don't want you to get blindsided again like you did the other day, and at least this time, I'm not driving 200 miles just to tell you something you already know."

I had to smile at that, and I supposed I appreciated him giving me the heads-up, although it still seemed like an odd thing for us to be talking about. "Would it bother you if something did happen between me and Jason?"

His lips tightened just a fraction. "It's not really any of my business, like you said."

At least we agreed on that. "Well, this is just a business lunch anyway, but thanks. I think. I'll see you later."

He gave me a nod and turned back to his computer while I headed to the restroom to freshen up for my lunch, which had suddenly gotten a little bit more interesting.

Chapter Six

~**Cam**~

Sitting at my desk for lunch after Tonia left proved impossible. The scent of her perfume still lingered in the air, and the thought of her and Jason having lunch together refused to leave me alone. She seemed genuinely surprised when I told her I thought he might be interested in her, so I had to assume he hadn't made any move yet, but how long that would last, I couldn't guess.

Maybe I shouldn't have said anything; it honestly wasn't my business, as she said, and I had kept my mouth shut the week before after Jason and I first talked about it. Still, after what happened with Bradyn on Friday and after the time we'd spent together in general on the weekend, I felt protective of her, whether she thought I should or not.

I couldn't just turn my feelings on and off like she seemed to be so good at doing.

Rather than sitting inside and stewing over things, I went for a walk instead, breathing in the fresh air as the warm noon sun shone down. Just a few blocks took me to Discovery Green, a green space filled with other people in business attire looking for a break from their work. Work had nothing to do with my restlessness, though. The session with Tonia that morning had been interesting and helpful. As I told her, she really knew her stuff, and though I couldn't help but be impressed, it didn't surprise me. With her drive and talent, she was always going to be a success, no matter what she put her mind to.

That part had all gone better than I expected. As I reflected back over the morning with the sun baking into my skin, I figured I just needed to do a better job of putting the personal stuff aside, since she couldn't have made it much clearer that, despite what happened on Friday night, she didn't see us as anything more than acquaintances. Friday had been a blip, and the sooner I accepted that, the better for both of us. The fresh air helped to clear my head and give me a sense of purpose; I could make it through the rest of the month without it getting weird.

When I returned to the office, Jason had returned to his office, talking to his assistant, Marianne, while I could see Tonia sitting in Jeremy's office just as she had been in mine that morning. The lunch hadn't lasted too long, so maybe that meant it hadn't gone all that well. Or maybe it just meant Tonia was on top of her time, as usual.

More importantly, why did I care?

As soon as I got back to my own office, I closed my door so that I wouldn't have to hear her laugh drifting in, and to my great relief, the rest of the afternoon went quickly as I got caught up on things from this morning and started to put a few of Tonia's suggestions in place. Time went so fast that when someone knocked on my door, I was surprised to see the clock saying five o'clock already.

"Come in," I called out, expecting to see one of my colleagues there to say goodnight, but instead, Tonia stood on the other side.

She looked calm and cool and as poised as ever. "Do you have a minute?"

"Sure." I hadn't expected to see her again that day, nor did I expect her to close the door behind her when she walked in, and against all logic and reason, my heart began to beat a little faster.

I couldn't help flashing back to that brief, drunken kiss at the bar in Corpus Christi, and as I did, I could almost taste her again. The alcohol mingled with her own sweet flavour, the scent of her perfume brought up a thousand memories from happier times and the way that her lips were somehow both soft and demanding at the same time drew me in just as much as it always had.

Though I knew just how unlikely it would be, I couldn't help wondering what I would do if she walked straight over to me and kissed me again right there at my desk. Based on the surge of energy that ran through my body, I had to admit the thought wasn't an entirely unpleasant one.

My surprise only grew when, after closing the door, she did march straight over to me. Unfortunately, the look on her face had nothing in common with desire.

"What the hell are you trying to pull, Cam?" She planted her hands on my desk, leaning across it to get as close to me as she could, so I couldn't look anywhere but directly at her. Though she didn't shout, she may as well have. She sounded angry enough. "Did you really think you're funny?"

My heart continued to pound, but confusion had replaced anticipation as its fuel. "I don't know what you're talking about, Sugar."

"Don't you 'sugar' me! I'm talking about you standing in this room just a few hours ago and telling me that Jason Barnly is interested in me. If you thought that would be funny, I can assure you that you're wrong."

Nothing she had just said made things any clearer. "You're going to have to back up to the station and let me board this train of thought."

Her glare made it clear she didn't find me charming at that moment. "You told me that Jason is interested in me," she repeated slowly, as if I were hard of hearing.

"Yeah, I got that part. It's the next bit that lost me. Why don't you sit down and tell me what happened?"

I gestured towards the chair behind her, but she stayed where she'd planted herself, not yielding an inch.

At least she started to explain herself. "We went out for lunch and after what you said, I took his behaviour for flirting. He's a nice guy, so I flirted back."

Jealousy twisted in my stomach. As much as I wished something else caused my discomfort, I had to be honest: I was jealous of my boss for flirting with my ex-girlfriend.

"We were having a nice time, and I started to think there might really be something there, *only* thought because *you* told me he was interested. So, I asked him if he wanted to grab a drink after work."

She asked *him* out? I groaned internally as her words sank in. *Nice work, Cam.* In trying to protect her, I'd managed to shove her straight into his arms. It had been a while since I'd screwed something up quite this badly.

'Round about six years, actually.

I still didn't understand exactly why she was so angry, though, until she got to the kicker. "And do you know what he said?"

She paused there as if she actually expected me to answer, and I could only hold up my hands. "I'm pretty sure I don't."

She didn't look like she believed me, but she told me anyway. "He said I'm a 'very nice' woman and he was flattered, but he thought it would be better to keep our relationship professional. Which is all I ever intended it to be in the first place if *you* hadn't put the idea in my head that he was interested in more!"

Her voice raised over the final sentences until she *was* almost shouting, and my eyes quickly flitted to the door, making sure it had been firmly closed. That seemed to remind her where we were, and pushing herself off my desk at last, she stood back up and took a step back.

"I might have seriously damaged my reputation here, and for what? So you could have a laugh at my expense?"

Anger still lingered in Tonia's eyes but hurt had joined it, and finally, I understood what she thought happened. She thought I set her up, but nothing could be further from the truth. Jason told me he liked her! Or at least... well, to be honest, when I thought back on it, I realized he only mentioned being interested in *someone* in the office.

Who else would he mean? Unless...

The image came back to me of passing his office after lunch and seeing his assistant speaking with him and the warm smile he gave her, and I groaned out loud, not bothering to try to keep it in. "Ah, damnit, Sugar. I might have got the wrong end of the stick."

"Might have?" she demanded, folding her arms across her chest.

Apparently, I would have to do better than that. "Look, he told me he's interested in someone here in the office but didn't know if it would be appropriate for him to act on it. I thought he meant you. It was an honest mistake."

"When he never used my name? Why would you assume that?" She still didn't sound like she believed me.

"Well, you're beautiful and funny and smart, and why the hell wouldn't he mean you? I didn't see who else it could be."

Her arms remained crossed but some of the tension had started to leave her shoulders. "There are at least ten other women I've seen working here. It never crossed your mind that it might be one of them?"

How could I explain that to me, none of them held a candle to her, without it sounding like the worst kind of line? "Obviously, I didn't think it through that much. I wasn't trying to set you up, honestly. I didn't expect you to go out and act on it right away, and I sure as hell didn't expect him to say no."

Out of the whole mess, that surprised me most of all, just as much as it relieved me. Didn't he see just how much of a catch she was? My boss must be an idiot.

"I'm sorry," I added, since she deserved an apology. That had to have been a bruise to her pride, whether I meant to do it or not.

Finally, her arms uncrossed. "Nothing is ever simple where you're concerned."

I knew that feeling all too well. "Ditto, Sugar."

When I called her by her pet name that time, she didn't correct me. Her lips twitched, just a little, as she took another step back. "Well, I guess the work day's over, and there is definitely a wine glass with my name on it at home. Apparently, my evening's free since I don't have a date."

Though I tried not to, I couldn't help imagining what Tonia Callahan's apartment looked like. Her kitchen would be all neatly organized and labeled, I would bet, and her closet colour-coded. And her bed...

Another rush of what could only be called desire ran through me at the thought of her bed, and I had to grit my teeth to stop it from showing.

I wanted her to ask me over to share a glass of wine with her. I wanted us to be able to sit and laugh about this misunderstanding, as we would have done back in the old days.

I wanted to go pin her against the wall and kiss her until she knew I would never do anything to intentionally hurt her.

Never again.

I didn't do any of that, though. Calling on the calm I'd tried so hard to find over my lunch outside, I simply said goodnight and watched as she walked away.

~**Tonia**~

Cam's explanation that he didn't set me up to make a fool of myself with Jason Barnly on purpose helped to ease the sting of my embarrassment a little, but only a little. As I settled down with a glass of wine on my apartment balcony, I still mostly felt like an idiot.

Seeing things through the lens that Cam's words had given me, I mistook Jason's banter for hitting on me, when he had only meant to be friendly. He probably thought I was desperate and unprofessional, the complete opposite of the impression I'd been trying to make. My dreams of dozens of recommendations coming from this particular job seemed to be disintegrating before my eyes.

As I sat there inhaling my Chardonnay, it would be fair to say I felt rather sorry for myself, but it only took one text to smarten me right up.

Today's treatment is done, she's resting now. If you're not busy tonight, would you mind picking me up some clean clothes? I haven't been home in three days. Dex.

Immediately, I put my half-drank glass of wine down and grabbed my purse. Nothing worked as well as being reminded what real problems looked like to help put my self-pity in perspective.

Close proximity to a department store had been one of the reasons I'd chosen my apartment building, so I headed there first, picking out some jeans and t-shirts, fresh socks and underwear, and some pajama pants for my brother too. While there, I also grabbed some steamy romance books for Shawna, figuring she could tease Dex and make him read them to her, as well as some of her favourite perfume and candy.

Laden down with bags, I headed back to my building to grab my truck, but I found my path blocked by a woman standing outside the door, staring at the list of tenant names on the entry panel.

"Are you looking for someone in particular?" I asked, partly to be helpful but mostly to move her out of the way.

As she turned to answer me, her eyes widened in surprise. "Oh. Tonia, hi. Actually, I'm looking for you."

She looked vaguely familiar to me but I couldn't place her. Obviously, she had no such trouble identifying me. "Can I help you?"

An amused smile pulled at her lips. "You don't recognize me, do you?"

I didn't, and my bags were getting heavier by the second. "I'm sorry, I don't, and I'm kind of in a hurry..."

"Here, let me help." Without waiting for my agreement, she took some of the bags from my hands. "You need to get your keys out, I suppose."

I did, but I still didn't know who this woman was and why she was holding my brother's pants. "What can I help you with?" I repeated as I fished my keys out of my pocket.

"I'm Marley Stevens."

The name hit me like a bucket of ice water dumped over my head, and as soon as I got the door open, I grabbed my bags back from her. "Of course you are. I see it now."

Now that she said it, I couldn't believe I'd missed it. I had spent those last few weeks before graduation hyper-aware of her in the hallways of the school. We weren't in any of the same classes, thank God, but even seeing her in the hall made my blood boil. She always slunk away when she noticed me, never having the guts to say anything to my face.

Her face had a more angular look and she had her hair cut shorter, but beyond that, the woman in front of me was undeniably the same woman.

What in the world would be she doing there? It couldn't be a coincidence that she turned up on my door right when Cam had reentered my life.

She quickly confirmed that coincidence played no part in it. "I know you probably don't want to talk to me but I think it's time we had a conversation. There are things you ought to know, things that Cam's too stubborn to tell you himself, and if you're going to be working together, it might help. Can we talk, please?"

I'd had just about enough of dredging up the past in the last few days. "Unfortunately, I'm on my way out."

"But... you just got home," she reminded me, sounding confused.

"And now I'm leaving again." I started to walk towards the staircase down to the parking garage, but she followed after me.

"Please, Tonia. I'm not in town very often, and it took a lot of hyping myself up to come here."

She still lived in Sandy Creek as far as I knew, still lived in that same house where I saw her and Cam together. I never went down that street if I could help it.

"You should have called first," I pointed out before playing my trump card. "My brother's wife is in the hospital and I'm on my way over there to bring them a few things, so if you don't mind..."

That got through to her, as I hoped it would. "Oh, I heard about Shawna. I'm so sorry. Mrs Armstrong told Mary Beth Livingstone, who told the ladies at the H-E-B."

Typical. Very few things stayed a secret in Sandy Creek.

"If you want some company..."

"I don't." The woman could not take a hint, apparently. "Look, Marley, high school was a long time ago. I've moved on, and I'm pretty sure Cam has too. If he doesn't want you to talk to me, then maybe you shouldn't."

I wrenched the door to the stairwell open, intent on making my grand exit, but her next words pulled me up short. "He wanted to tell you, at least back then."

Against my better judgement, I paused at the top of the stairs. "Tell me what?"

"About everything. About him spending time with me and why. He didn't want you to get the wrong idea. The only reason he didn't was because I begged him not to say anything."

That didn't sound like much of an excuse to me. "Well, he made that choice. He was a big boy, Marley; if he really wanted to tell me, he could have. Now, I really do have to go."

She didn't follow me, thankfully, but she did call down the stairs after me. "I'm in Houston until Wednesday. Let me know if you change your mind about talking."

She didn't say how I could let her know, but she didn't have to. I just had to put the word out to anyone in Sandy Creek and they would make sure she knew. At that moment, however, I had no intention of doing any such thing.

By the time I got to the hospital, I had completely focused back on my brother, pushing all my own juvenile drama to the back of my mind. I texted Dex when I arrived and he said Shawna had woken up so I should go straight to her room.

The cancer ward never felt like a very happy place to be and that night, it felt even more depressing than usual. The grim looks on the faces of other visitors reminded me how bad things could get and the smell of disinfectant made me feel slightly nauseous, but the sight that greeted me when I arrived at Shawna's room still warmed my heart. Dex sat in a chair beside the bed, holding Shawna's hand, his head close to hers as they laughed over some private joke. Exhaustion was written across both of their faces, but it faded in the light of the affection they so obviously had for each other.

Every woman deserved someone who looked at them the way my brother looked at his wife.

Those kinds of words would never come out of my mouth, though. My relationship with my brother usually avoided any kind of overtly sentimental display, so I said something completely different to announce my arrival: "You both look like shit."

Women like Shawna and me didn't want things sugarcoated, and she smiled at me as I walked in, not taking offense in the least.

"At least I have an excuse," she said, her voice softer and scratchier than usual, before she gestured at her husband. "I'm not sure what his problem is."

Dex scratched at the stubble along his jawline that had gone well beyond a five o'clock shadow. "What'd'ya expect when I haven't showered in four days?"

"Ugh, your poor wife!" I exclaimed. "She shouldn't have to deal with your stench on top of everything else. Here, take these and go shower right now. I'll stay until you're back."

Shawna nodded in agreement and Dex wearily got to his feet, leaning down to place a kiss on her forehead. "I'll be back real soon, baby." Coming around the foot of the bed, he took the bags of clothes from my hands. "Thanks, Tonia."

"Of course." I wrinkled my nose as he got closer. "You should have called me sooner."

He gave me just a hint of his usual smile before leaving the room, and I quickly took his spot on the chair next to Shawna's bed.

"I've got a few things for you too. If there's anything else you need, just let me know."

She thanked me and took a look through the bag, laughing when I told her why I'd bought the books. When she'd looked through it all, she put the bag to the side and turned back to me. "So, what's going on with you and Cam?"

I tried not to groan. "Not you too. What have my sisters said?"

"Nothing," she promised, and laughed again when I raised my eyebrows. "Honestly, it wasn't them. Dex told me you guys are working together and that he came here with you on Friday night. So, the question stands: what's going on?"

"Wouldn't you rather read some of your new books instead?" I suggested. "It would be a lot more entertaining, and have a happier ending too."

She gave me an unimpressed look. "I asked because I want to know. And I'm pretty sure you have to do as I say, those are the rules of the cancer ward. The one in the bed has the final say."

She had me there, so I gave her the short version: "He's working at the company I've been contracted with this month. We ended up having some drinks together on Friday night, as colleagues, and he was there when I got Dex's text, so he came with me to the hospital. That's it."

Her lips pursed in disapproval at my weak summary. "Try again."

With a sigh, I backed up and told her the whole story. She didn't interrupt but I could practically see her making mental notes at different things she wanted to come back to, and I noticed her trying not to laugh when I told her about my lunch with Jason.

When I added the part about Marley turning up at my apartment an hour ago, she shook her head. "I honestly don't know which of you two is more stubborn."

"Me or Marley?" I asked in confusion.

"You or *Cam*," she clarified. "Though if I had to put money on it, I'd bet on you."

"I'm not stubborn," I protested. "At least not where he's concerned. I'm just standing up for myself. He hurt me, and he doesn't get to get away with that."

"Forgiveness isn't about letting someone off the hook," she argued back. "It's about finding a way to move forward, but neither of you have done that. You're both still stuck in the past."

"I am not." I realized I sounded like a child, but she had really struck a nerve. "I *have* moved on and that's why I don't need to talk about it anymore, especially not with 'the other woman'."

Shawna had a different interpretation. "You don't want to talk to Marley because you're afraid."

"I am not afraid of her," I scoffed, leaning back in my seat and crossing my arms. Marley had far more reason to be scared of me than I was of her.

"I didn't say you were. You're afraid of finding out that there was more to what happened back then than you let yourself think. It's all been black and white in your mind, and you're afraid that if you let in some shades of grey, it's going to mess up the whole picture. And most of all, I think you're afraid that somewhere deep down, you still care about him."

I could protest again but there didn't seem any point. She'd already made up her mind.

"Life's short, Tonia," she added bluntly. "If you're really over this, then go and talk to Marley and let her move on too. And if you're not over it, then you should deal with it now. It's been six years already. What if something happened to Cam? What if, God forbid, he ends up in a bed like this, or worse, and you realize that you missed your chance? Don't put it off any longer. If there's anything this whole shitshow has taught me, it's that. That's why we're still having everyone over to the gallery on Friday. Life goes on, and I don't plan on wasting a minute of it. Don't waste yours either, Tonia. Let it go for real, or face up to it, but don't just pretend it doesn't bother you when it clearly does."

That impassioned speech seemed to sap the last of her energy and she sank back into her pillows just as Dex returned, looking much fresher and smelling a lot better too.

"What's wrong, baby?" he quickly asked, sitting down on the bed on Shawna's other side and picking up her hand.

"Nothing," Shawna assured him, giving him a smile. "Just trying to talk some sense into your sister. You know how tiring that can be."

He nodded in agreement as I rolled my eyes. "Alright, it's clearly two against one now and I don't like those odds. I'll leave you two in peace."

I leaned down to give Shawna a hug, trying to ignore how frail she seemed again. How had I not noticed it before? The happy bride dancing at her wedding six months earlier seemed like a distant memory.

"Promise me you'll think about it," she whispered in my ear, and I nodded.

"I will. I promise."

As I made my way back to my apartment, that was exactly what I did, and the more I thought about it, the more I had to admit she might just have a point. What did I have to be afraid of? Nothing Marley could say would change the facts, so what would it hurt to talk to her?

By the time I got back to my apartment, I had made up my mind, and I quickly sent my mom a text. *Could you get someone a message for me?*

Chapter Seven

~**Cam**~

After Tonia left my office, I packed up to head home, but as I made my way past Jason's office, I noticed he was still there. Since he seemed to be alone and not on his phone, I changed course and headed to his door instead.

"You got a minute?" I asked as I rapped lightly on the open door.

He flashed me a welcoming smile as he leaned back from his computer. "Sure. What's up?"

I closed the door behind me and went to take a seat across from him. Since I hadn't planned this, I didn't know exactly how to begin, but I felt like I owed it to Tonia to take some responsibility for what happened between them today. I might make things worse by sticking my nose into it even further, but hopefully, that wouldn't be the case. Surely, I must have reached my maximum number of screw-ups in one week by that point.

"I just had a chat with Tonia Callahan, and I understand things got a little awkward between you two at lunch."

Jason grimaced in confirmation. "I hope I didn't make her feel bad. It took me by surprise, and I don't think of her like that. I want to keep the whole relationship professional."

"She understands completely," I assured him. "And the thing is... she only asked you for a drink because she thought you were flirting with her, and she only thought *that* because I told her you liked her."

"What?" My boss definitely didn't look impressed with that, as I suspected he wouldn't be. It would have been easier for me to keep my mouth shut, but I didn't want him to have the wrong idea about Tonia. That wouldn't be fair when I'd set her down the wrong path to begin with.

"I misunderstood our conversation last week about relationships in the office. I thought you were talking about Tonia since she showed up that day."

"And so, you told her that?" Jason looked less impressed with me by the second. "That whole conversation was confidential. Even if I *had* been talking about her, which I wasn't, you shouldn't have said anything."

"I get that, I do," I promised. "Problem is, I always seem to lose my head when Tonia's around."

"Always?" He repeated the word curiously, and I knew I would have to come clean.

"She and I go back a long way. If it had been *anyone* else, I wouldn't have said it, and even with her, I probably wouldn't have said it if it weren't for what happened on Friday."

I told him the whole story, almost, explaining how Tonia and I used to go out back in high school, how we had a bad breakup and had avoided each other since, and how I overreacted on Friday and went down to Corpus Christi. He might not have followed along with everything, but by the time I finished, at least he looked a little more sympathetic.

"You should have told me you knew her," he pointed out.

"I know. I should have done a lot of things, but like I said, she has this effect on me where I seem to turn into a complete idiot. I hoped I'd outgrown it, but after this week, I don't think it's going to happen. I think I just have to accept it."

That made him smile, thankfully.

"And I just really wanted you to know that her asking you out today wasn't typical for her. She's very professional. I think I just got in her head with what I said, and I don't want you to have the wrong impression."

"You still care about her." He phrased it as a statement rather than a question, but I nodded anyway.

"Yeah. Not in a 'I want to get back together' way, but I still think she's a great person and I really didn't mean to mess things up for her, or for you either. So please, don't hold it against her, and I'll just crawl back to my office and hide for the rest of the month."

He cracked another smile. "That won't be necessary, Cam. Thanks for clearing things up, though. I appreciate a guy who takes responsibility for his mistakes."

"I've had a fair bit of practice at that." The conversation seemed to be drawing to a close so I got to my feet. "Have a good night, Jason."

"You too." I almost made it to the door before he spoke again. "Hey, if you're not busy tomorrow, I've got this industry party I'm meant to go to. I was going to ask... well, it doesn't really matter, but the point is, I haven't asked anyone yet, and I think it's too late now. Do you mind coming along for backup?"

A moment earlier, I'd felt lucky just to be leaving with my job intact, so I quickly jumped at the opportunity. "Yeah, of course. What's the dress code?"

"I'll send you the details. Good night, Cam."

I couldn't help smiling as I left the office. A chance to mingle with some industry bigwigs and impress my boss at the same time, even after making a fool of myself? Maybe my luck had finally started to change where Tonia was concerned.

I had another two hours with Tonia the next afternoon but she kept strictly to business and so did I. She didn't bring up Jason and I didn't mention that I spoke to him. After everyone else went home, I changed into the slightly more formal suit I'd brought for the night, and Jason and I got a cab over to the Sam Houston Race Park where the event was being held.

"My dad's going to be here," Jason confided in me. "But I really want to show people that Barnly Oil is its own business, and I'm not just riding on my dad's coattails."

I understood that completely. "I've got your back," I promised.

The night passed quickly as we did our best to work the room. Whenever anyone had questions about our projections and operations, I stepped in to provide answers, and I could tell that Jason appreciated having me there. The night turned out to be a good one for both of us.

Just as things were winding down and the drinks we'd had were starting to kick in, a couple of women approached us, obviously interested in more than just a chat.

"That's my cue to leave," Jason told me. "Enjoy the rest of your night and charge your cab home to the company."

He walked away before I could protest, leaving me with the two women.

"You look familiar," the darker-haired one said to me with an inviting smile. "I'm sure I've seen you somewhere before."

"That's possible. I do go outside once in a while."

I hadn't thought it was all that funny, but they both laughed like they'd never heard anything wittier.

"I think you live in my building," she continued, naming the address of my apartment building.

"Yeah, I guess I do." I didn't recognize her, but then, I had made a resolution not to get involved with anyone in my building, so it didn't really surprise me. "And I actually better get heading back there now. I've got work in the morning."

"I'm about to leave too," she told me quickly, though it hadn't seemed that way a moment earlier. "We can split a cab. It's better for the environment."

I couldn't think of a good reason to say no, so I waited while she went to the restroom, said goodnight to her friend and picked up her coat from the coat check before we headed out to the waiting taxis together.

We had a friendly enough chat during the cab ride home; a little flirty, but not too much, but I simply wasn't interested. Even if she didn't live in my building, which made her off-limits in my mind, I just wasn't feeling it. Something in the back of my head suggested that had something to do with Tonia, but I quickly shut that voice down. Tonia hadn't been an option for me for a long time, and I couldn't let her hold me back from anything.

There just wasn't any spark there, I told myself. You had chemistry with someone or you didn't, and between the two of us, I felt none.

I paid for the taxi when we arrived and helped her out of the car to be polite, and she quickly grabbed hold of my arm and held onto it as we walked into the lobby. Just as I wondered how I could manage to get rid of her in a nice way before she invited herself back to my room, an unexpected voice called out my name.

"Cam?"

~Tonia~

The reply from Marley came through on my phone, ironically, just as I left Cam's office. After my conversation with Shawna the night before and the prospect of speaking to Marley later, I wanted to keep things with Cam strictly business-like, and I'd done so. He hadn't attempted to draw me into any other kind of conversation either, so it seemed for the time being, at least, we were on the same page.

Marley's text said that she would be available for a late dinner tonight if I wanted to eat, but I responded and said that a drink would be better. I couldn't see the point of being stuck with her for a whole dinner. How much could she possibly have to tell me?

She was busy until nine, so we met just afterwards at a bar downtown, not too far from the Barnly Oil offices. I still had my work clothes on, a pretty white blouse with a blank pencil skirt, while she wore jeans and a flannel shirt, looking out of place among the other businesspeople. It didn't seem to bother her, though, as we found a quiet table in the back and ordered our drinks.

"I'm glad you changed your mind," she began as the waitress walked away to put our orders in. "I've told Cam so many times to simply tell you what happened, but he keeps refusing. You know how stubborn he is."

Hearing that they were still in touch, that she talked to him 'so many times' and her bringing up his stubbornness like we could laugh about it together did nothing to improve my mood. I hadn't gone there to catch up or to make friends. I wanted to hear what she had to tell me, and nothing more.

"I didn't even know you and Cam were friends," I told her bluntly. "In fact, I asked him straight out if he knew you and he said no."

She winced at both my tone and the accusation in my words. "Well, as I mentioned briefly the other day, I asked him not to tell you. And the truth is we didn't really know each other very well until a few weeks before prom. I was a nobody at school and he was... well, he was Cam Bailey, with you as his girlfriend. People like the two of you didn't pay attention to people like me."

I didn't think that was fair. I may have been popular, but I had never been a snob about it. In such a small town, there weren't really cliques, not like there were in city schools. "You weren't in our year," I pointed out to her. "And you didn't play sports or take part in any of the clubs. When would we have gotten to know each other?"

Her fingers drummed nervously on the table. "I know, I'm not trying to... shoot, this is coming out wrong already. I'm not trying to say you were mean to me or anything like that. I just knew you didn't notice me and neither did Cam, not until he caught me at work one day."

"Caught you?" My brow furrowed as I tried to figure out what she meant. Cam had worked at the local grocery store during high school. He'd been great at it, like he was at most things; charming the older women when they came to do their shopping, negotiating deals with local suppliers, and helping the manager completely revolutionize their bookkeeping. He'd even been offered the assistant manager job at 17, but he had always had bigger dreams than that. Dreams like being the CFO of an oil company, for one.

Marley nodded to assure me I'd heard her correctly. "He saw me shoving some fruit into my bag without paying for it. He could have called me out right then and there, but he didn't. He waited until I'd left and he followed me. You know that park across the street from the store?"

Of course I did.

"He caught up to me there and asked why I'd done it. I was terrified he would report me or call the cops or whatever, but that wasn't what he wanted. He just wanted to know why I felt I needed to take it."

That sounded exactly like Cam, or at least the Cam I used to know. Based on what I'd seen in the past week, I had to guess he still behaved the same way.

"I didn't want to tell him. I hadn't told anyone about my situation and I didn't know him at all. I remember my hands shaking, I was so nervous, but he stayed kind and encouraging. He made it feel like it would be okay to tell him."

Again, I knew exactly what she meant, so I simply nodded.

"So, I told him the truth. My mom had gotten really sick the week before and my dad brought her all the way to Houston, to a clinic that would take uninsured people. We didn't have a lot of money and we didn't have health insurance. My dad had been on disability for years ever since he hurt his back, and he hated the idea of people knowing just how poor we were, so he took her as far away as he could go. When they got there, they found out that she had advanced liver cancer. They couldn't have done much to treat it even if we had money for the treatment, which we didn't."

Immediately, my mind flashed back to Shawna in her hospital bed the previous night, and the way Marley had expressed her sympathy over hearing that Shawna's cancer had returned. Apparently, she had personal experience with it, and cancer sucked, we could agree on that much.

"Anyway, my dad couldn't come home. We didn't have the money for gas to keep driving back and forth, so I got left on my own, with no money left for groceries. My hunger got the better of me and that's why I took the food from the store. I begged Cam not to tell anyone, even though he had every right to. I didn't want my parents to be worried about that on top of everything else."

They should have been a little *more* worried about their daughter having food to eat, I couldn't help thinking, but I kept my mouth shut, letting her speak as the waitress brought our drinks over. Neither of us touched the glasses as she continued her story.

"He said he wouldn't report me, and though I offered to give the fruit back, he told me to keep it. He went back to work and I went home, and later that night, someone knocked on my door. I didn't plan to answer since I was there on my own, but Cam called through the door, and when I opened it, he stood there with two bags of groceries he'd bought for me."

Just like he had at my brother's wedding, Cam always came to the rescue; he couldn't help it. It seemed to be in his blood, and I could appreciate the kindness and thoughtfulness of the gesture. What I didn't understand was why he never told me about it, and how it led from that one selfless act to him taking her to prom.

Marley did her best to explain that next. "He wanted to tell the ladies at church, he said there would be so many people who would help me out if they only knew, but I knew my dad would be furious. He'd always been ridiculously stubborn and proud, and he didn't want handouts from anyone, even when we could have used them. So, I begged Cam to keep it a secret, even from you. The way his face fell when I asked him that, Tonia, if you'd have seen it... I could tell he'd never kept anything from you before."

"You had no right to ask him that," I pointed out, though I kept my tone soft. I felt bad for her; who wouldn't? I wasn't a monster, but it still didn't explain everything.

"I didn't see another choice," she told me bluntly. "The Callahans were exactly the type of people my dad didn't want feeling bad for us. If Cam told you, other people might find out. I trusted him, barely, but I didn't know you. I only knew the perfect girl at school that everyone else wanted to be like."

I ignored that comment to return to her narrative. "How long did this go on for?"

Marley took a sip from her drink to wet her mouth. She'd been doing almost all the talking up to that point. "Just over two weeks. He came over almost every night to make sure I had what I needed, and he even slept over a few times, on the couch in the living room, because he felt bad about me sleeping there on my own. He was just a really, really decent guy, and I began to think... well, I began to hope, I guess, that something else lay behind all of this attention he gave me other than just friendship."

We were getting to the heart of things. This must have been when things took a turn, and I did my best to brace myself for it.

"My dad called and said that they'd been told my mom only had a couple of weeks left. He put her on the phone with me and she was so sad, talking about all the things she'd never get to see, like my wedding or even my prom, and that's when I had the idea."

"What idea?" I asked uneasily. So far, Cam hadn't done a single thing wrong in her story other than not telling me the truth, and I was still waiting for the other shoe to drop.

"I decided to..." She trailed off, closing her eyes in pain or embarrassment, I couldn't tell which. Maybe both. "I asked Cam to take me to prom so that I could take pictures for my mom and show them to her when I went up to visit the following weekend. My dad said he would come and bring me up to say goodbye, and I thought it might make her happy to see the pictures, and I thought... well, I hoped that maybe if Cam took me to prom, if people saw us together and we had a good time, that maybe he would admit he felt something for me too."

The sinking feeling in my stomach got worse. "*You* asked *him* to prom?" When she nodded, I quickly followed up with another question. "And he just said yes?"

Marley shook her head vehemently. "No, of course not. He told me he would be going with you, of course, but that he could ask one of his friends to take me and that we could all go as a group. Looking back, I can see how hard he tried to make me a reasonable offer, but at the time, I was really shy and I didn't want to go with someone I didn't know, not to mention that I really wanted to go with Cam, so I refused. I got really emotional about it, and I'm... I'm ashamed now when I think about it. It's not something I'm proud of, but basically, I blackmailed him with my dying mother to take me to the prom instead of you."

Oh, Cam. Sweet, helpful, unable-to-say-no Cam. Was that the scene I had seen through her bedroom window, with her ranting and raving and him embracing her afterwards?

"So, nothing happened between you before prom?" I clarified, just to make sure I had understood her correctly. "You never slept together?"

Marley blushed as she shook her head. "Absolutely not. He never even kissed me. He hugged me a few times, but only in a friendly way. And even after you broke up, nothing happened then either. He just didn't think of me that way, ever."

I really couldn't believe it. Why didn't he tell me any of this? Why didn't he tell me before I heard it from someone else, and why didn't he tell me afterwards, when he saw how heartbroken I was?

"He asked me not to say anything about prom until he had a chance to talk to you," Marley continued. "He stayed at my house that night and he went home in the morning to shower and get ready, and he planned to go and talk to you as soon as you got to school, but I... I let it slip. I got to school early and ran into Kara Beckett, making her usual backhand comments about how no one would ever take someone like me to prom, and I just said it. I didn't mean to; at least, I don't think I did. I just wanted to see the look on her face, but then of course she ran off and told you, and... well, you know the rest."

I certainly did. I knew what I said, and I knew what he said, and at that moment, I had a few more things I wanted to say to Cameron Bailey.

"Do you know where he lives?" I asked Marley, and her eyes widened in surprise.

"Cam?"

Who else would I be talking about? "Yes, Cam. You said you talk to him. Do you know where he lives?"

She nodded, still looking confused. "It's not far from here."

"Give me the address."

"Are you going to tell him I told you..."

I didn't care what promise she'd broken or why he'd asked her to stay silent about it in the first place. "Just give me the address!"

Wincing, she pulled out her phone and texted the address to me while I grabbed a ten-dollar bill from my wallet and slammed it down on the table to pay for my untouched drink.

"I'm really sorry, Tonia," she said as the text buzzed on my phone. "I didn't mean to hurt you. Like I said, I didn't even know you..."

I walked away before she could finish. I could apologize to her for my abrupt departure later, but my mind had already moved on, completely focused on what I planned to do next.

It didn't take me long to find Cam's building, and I had to admit to being impressed. He was obviously doing just fine for himself, if I hadn't already guessed that from his office at Barnly Oil. Silence greeted me when I buzzed up to his apartment, but someone else came out while I stood there waiting, so I grabbed the door and let myself in. Unfortunately, the elevator required a keycard to gain access to his floor, so just going and knocking on his door didn't seem to be an option.

The lobby contained a few comfortable-looking chairs, so I went to sit on one of them to send him a text, but before I could figure out what I wanted to say, I saw him come in, flooding my whole body in nervous anticipation. He wore a suit, but not the one he'd been wearing in the office earlier that day, and he had a dark-haired woman hanging off his arm, looking a little tipsy as they made their way to the elevator.

A reasonable woman would have said nothing. He hadn't seen me, and if I just left, he would never have known I was there.

However, I never claimed to be reasonable.

"Cam?" I said his name as I got to my feet, and a look of dismay crossed his face as he turned around and saw me.

"Tonia?" He glanced back at the woman at his side. "This, uh, this isn't what it looks like."

I didn't care about that. I didn't care about the woman and what he may or may not have been about to do with her. What I cared about happened six long years ago.

"Why didn't you tell me?" I walked right up to him, so close the woman beside him had no choice but to step back. "All these years, you let me think you cheated on me. You broke my heart over something that wasn't even true."

Surprise, confusion and a touch of anger all flashed through his deep brown eyes. "How did you..." He quickly put it together, before he'd even finished asking the question. "You talked to Marley."

"I shouldn't have had to hear it from her. Why didn't you ever say anything, you complete and utter moron?!"

"Why didn't you trust me?" The bitterness in his voice bled through just as strong as mine did. "You want to talk about broken hearts? Why did you immediately jump to the worst conclusion rather than asking me if it was true? Why did you never once just ask me what happened?"

"I *did* ask you," I reminded him, my voice still sharp. The woman who had been with him had begun backing away, clearly deciding that whatever she might have been about to have with him wasn't worth it. "I asked you if you knew her and you looked me in the eyes and lied to me."

"Because it had nothing to do with you then," he pointed out. "Once you had been hurt, I would have explained it, if you'd ever just given me a goddamned chance to!"

I didn't even remember deciding to slap him, but suddenly my hand was raised. Suddenly, we were back at Dex's wedding, the hurt between us bubbling right there beneath the surface, but unlike that time, there in his apartment building, he saw it coming. His hand shot out to grab my arm, stopping me in my tracks, and when I tried to pull it back again, he wouldn't let go. His eyes burned into me, blazing with the fire that had always burned between us. In the next instant, his grip on my arm tightened as he pulled me close to him, and once again, my body took over.

Before I even knew what I was doing, my arms were around him and my lips were on his, kissing him like my life depended on it.

Chapter Eight

~**Cam**~

No words existed that could do justice to what went through my head when Tonia kissed me. The last minute had been a roller coaster ride of ups and downs and twists and turns. Whiplash would have been less traumatic.

When I first turned around and saw her standing there in the lobby of my building, with this other woman I'd just met on my arm, guilt had been my immediate gut reaction.

Which was *insane.*

I had nothing to feel guilty about. I hadn't been doing anything with that woman, and even if I had been, it didn't affect Tonia in any way. She had no problem going out to lunch with Jason, flirting with him and asking him out, so there was no earthly reason for me to feel bad about standing there with another woman, even if I had intended to take her up to my apartment, which I hadn't.

And yet, reason and logic didn't seem to matter; I felt guilty anyway and it frustrated the hell out of me.

It quickly became clear, however, that Tonia didn't care about the woman next to me. She didn't even spare her a glance as she marched over to me, her eyes full of fire and fury.

It took me a moment to piece together what happened: Marley must have finally caved after all this time and told Tonia the truth. I didn't know if Marley approached Tonia or Tonia approached Marley, and at that moment, I didn't particularly care. Tonia's anger erased every other concern from my mind. After all those years, she finally knew the truth and she *still* thought the fault was entirely mine? In her eyes, I couldn't see even a hint of that apology she still owed me.

It felt like déjà vu as we shouted at each other, again, just like we had in the school hallway that morning, and then she tried to slap me, again, like she had at Dex's wedding. Why did we keep going in circles? Shouting hadn't done us any good in the past and neither had physical aggression. Since we had nothing left to hide, we might as well deal with it, once and for all, and so I grabbed onto her, determined not to let her run away again.

Maybe I pulled her a little too close. Maybe she saw something in my eyes that I didn't even know was there.

Whatever the reason, she changed gears again, taking me completely by surprise as her lips connected with mine.

Her kiss didn't feel anything like the drunk, accidental kind of kiss we shared in Corpus Christi. It felt entirely intentional, determined, and filled with a passion and heat I hadn't experienced in a hell of a long time.

Tonia might run hot and cold, but when she was hot, she was *hot.* I hadn't met the woman yet who I could call her equal. She turned me on like no one else ever had.

The elevator doors slid open behind us as someone exited into the lobby, and almost before I knew what was happening, we'd stumbled into it, our lips still locked together.

"Your key," Tonia murmured against my skin, and for a moment, I had no idea what she meant. My brain seemed to be short circuiting and nothing made much sense, but eventually, I realized we were in an elevator going nowhere.

And she had just suggested we go to my apartment.

Desire and anticipation shot through me as I dug in my pocket for the keycard. I had to remove my lips from Tonia's long enough to swipe it over the sensor and hit the button for my floor, but as soon as I'd accomplished that, we were drawn back together, and I pressed her up against the mirrored wall, just as I'd imagined doing the day before in my office. My hands in her hair, I tugged it downwards just enough to make her look up at me, claiming her mouth again in a kiss both needy and possessive. In my office, I hadn't been sure how she'd react, but there in the sleek, confined space of the elevator, she grabbed hold of my hips and pulled them tighter towards her. My suit pants didn't hide much, and I knew she could feel just how hard I was, how hard she'd managed to make me in a matter of seconds.

Could this actually be happening? It sure as hell felt like it. A tiny voice in my head said to slow down, to talk things out first, but the rest of my body drowned it out, every inch of my physical being simply saying: *Yes. I want this.*

When we reached my floor, Tonia pushed me out of the elevator into the hall. "Which way?"

I honestly had to think about it for a minute, but eventually, I looped my arm around her waist and led her down the hallway to the left, our shoes sinking into the carpet as we walked past the abstract art on the walls, my eyes seeing nothing but the doorway ahead, desperate to get her inside.

"Do you want a drink or..." I started to ask once I'd closed the door behind us, but I didn't get a chance to finish before Tonia's body pressed against mine again. The smell of her and the taste of her was so familiar, and yet completely new at the same time. There in my apartment that belonged firmly to my new life, the past and present blended together in the best possible way.

"What does it feel like I want, Cam?" she teased me, pressing her hips up against me again, making me groan.

"Are you sure? I don't want us to regret..."

Once again, she cut me off, this time with her hand reaching between us to press against my straining erection. "Are you telling me I don't know what I want?"

Inhaling sharply, I shook my head. I knew better than that. "No, ma'am."

She grinned with that mischievous smile of hers that always brought me to my knees. "Good. Then where's the bedroom?"

Fuck, this really was happening.

With my heart pounding, sending all the blood it could to my eager cock, I took her down the hall to my room. As we walked in, she took a curious look around, nodding in approval. "Not bad, Cam."

Her approval meant a ridiculous amount to me. I shouldn't care what she thought of it, but of course I did. "The room looks a whole lot better with you in it, Sugar," I told her honestly.

The compliment made her smile as she stepped away from me and began to undo the buttons on her blouse, those buttons I'd tried so hard not to stare at in the office earlier that day, imagining what lay beneath them. I never thought I would actually get to see it.

"How's the view now?" she teased as she undid the last button and pulled the blouse open.

Though I'd seen her in just her bra before, at some point, surely the clock must reset. Seeing her in that moment felt new. The two experiences couldn't be compared, except that she looked equally amazing in both scenarios.

My tie had begun to choke me as I struggled to catch my breath, so I quickly pulled it off along with my suit jacket. At any moment, she might change her mind, or something might happen to blow apart this fragile peace, and I didn't want to give it a chance. No matter what might come afterwards, she wanted this, and I fucking wanted it too. We wanted each other, and if it would only be that one time, then so be it.

At least we'd have one more time.

My eagerness made her laugh as she watched me undress, but she was just as restless, tugging her blouse all the way off and pulling down her skirt while I made short work of the rest of my clothes. Nothing about our movements could be called slow or sensual. Everything felt hurried and frenzied, fuelled by an almost uncontrollable lust on both sides.

When we were finally naked, we both paused at last, taking a minute to simply look over each other, noting all the things that had changed and all the things that hadn't. It didn't take long for me to realize she was still the most beautiful woman I'd ever seen; maybe even more than before. She'd filled out from the girl I knew, her hips more curved, her breasts just a little bigger, but not enough that I didn't recognize every inch of her. I would have known her anywhere.

"How do you want this?" I asked her, my voice thick with longing. I had a few condoms in the drawer of my bedside table and I grabbed one out of habit. I'd never had sex without one, not with her and not with anyone. My responsible side wouldn't let me.

"Like in Dallas," came her reply, and my cock jumped right when I tried to roll the condom on as I realized exactly what she meant.

We'd gone to Dallas on a school trip in senior year. There were chaperones to keep the boys and girls apart, but we found a way around it, grabbing our chance to sneak off together at the hotel. We found a small utility closet, barely big enough for the two of us, and full of teenage hormones, I took her up against the wall as we tried not to make a sound.

There was no need to be quiet in my apartment though, so as soon as I had the condom on, I walked over to her and kissed her again. My hands ran down the smooth, toned skin of her back until I cupped her ass, and with the desperation of a starving man, I grabbed hold of her and lifted her up as she wrapped her legs around me. With her hips grinding against me and her slick entrance rubbing against my cock, I took a few steps forward until her back hit the wall.

"You're really sure?" I asked her one last time, and when she kissed me again, I thrust straight into her for the first time in almost six years.

~Tonia~

"Oh my God!"

The words burst from my lips as Cam drove into me, filling me completely, and he let out a strangled laugh as he bottomed out, his hips pressed right against me. "You took the words right out of my mouth, Sugar. Fuck, that feels good."

He wasn't wrong. My body had been on fire ever since I kissed him down in the lobby, the throbbing, aching need growing stronger by the second as we staggered our way to his apartment.

I hadn't meant to kiss him; not really. My emotions were all over the place and I needed to let them out somehow. Kissing him might not have been the smartest way to do it, but when I did, and when I felt the answering passion and hunger in his kiss, it tipped the scales. All my anger, my disbelief, and my hurt that had been brought to the surface during the talk with Marley and all the memories that it stirred up all melted into a deep pool of lust. Rather than trying to pull myself out, I decided to sink down into it instead.

I wanted to drown in those deep brown eyes, even if only one more time. I wanted to remember how it felt when he was my whole world, and how he taught me things about my body I'd never known before. We'd learned so much together, shared so many firsts together, and sometimes, nothing compared to the original. Though I'd been with other men since, it had never felt quite the same.

Not that he looked exactly the same either. His body was firmer and more defined than it used to be, the result of working out in the gym downstairs, no doubt, and unless I imagined it, his cock looked bigger too. It certainly felt that way as it stretched me open, filling me up completely as it reached the deepest part of me, both soothing my ache and driving my desire for him even higher.

"This ain't gonna be soft and sweet, Tonia," he warned me, his eyes blazing with need, but that was fine with me. I didn't want soft. I wanted the hunger. I wanted to lose myself completely in the way he made me feel.

"Less talk and more action, Bailey," I egged him on, and my words had the desired effect. With his fingers digging into my ass, my back pressed against the wall, and my arms around his shoulders to keep my balance, he pulled out slowly, his cock dragging along my inner walls in exquisitely drawn-out pleasure before he slammed back into me again. "Fuck, yes!"

I wanted exactly that, and he didn't fail to deliver. Over and over, he thrust into me, hard and fast, grinding his hips into me so that he rubbed against my clit each time, and it didn't take long for my orgasm to build. Part of me couldn't believe we were really doing this, but a much bigger part of me loved every second of it.

"Oh... God... yes... Cam... fuck!"

The words came out of me disconnected, each like their own sentence, as the peak of my pleasure hit, and he slowed just enough to let me enjoy it. A wave of fulfillment crashed over me, followed by smaller swells, my body floating through my orgasm as he held me steady, but as soon as it calmed, he was ready for more.

His hands still holding me tight, he pulled back from the wall and carried me over to his bed. It looked like a good one, I couldn't help thinking even through my post-orgasmic haze, and when he placed me down on it, it felt firm beneath me. I could get a good night's sleep in that bed.

"On your hands and knees, Sugar," he instructed, and I hurried to comply. He remembered Dallas, and he remembered how much I enjoyed this position too, and I appreciated not having to spell it all out. He simply knew what I wanted.

Instead of resuming his earlier activity, however, he bent down instead, spreading my legs wider as he licked along my dripping hole.

"Fuck, you're just as sweet as I remembered," he muttered, and my body jolted in pleasure, both at the rough swipe of his tongue and the deep timbre of his voice. When he moved down to my swollen clit, kissing and sucking on it, my knees nearly buckled.

I thought I remembered how good it felt, but I'd been wrong. What I felt in that moment exceeded any of my memories. Every inch of me seemed to be tuned to him, responding to every action as if it were a secret song that only the two of us knew. Desire built up inside me again as his tongue and fingers continued to work me until I was trembling in need, and just before I came, he suddenly stopped and thrust his hard cock into me.

With that perfect mix of sensations, I came immediately, clamping down on him as he groaned in appreciation. "That's my girl," he murmured, and at that point, I wasn't about to argue.

With his hands holding my hips tight, he began to fuck me again, *hard* again, with one foot up on the bed to get the angle just right. He knew just where my g-spot was; he'd helped me find it, after all, and it definitely didn't seem like he'd forgotten how to get there.

His breath grew ragged as his own climax drew closer, and he reached down to rub my clit again, wanting me to come with him. "I know you've got one more for me tonight," he growled. "Give it to me, Tonia."

Fuck, fuck, fuck. That was the Cam I had missed the most. I had loved the sweet guy, the one who would give anyone the shirt off his back, the one who supported and loved me back, but the firm, sexy side of him had been the reason I fell for him so hard and completely. He knew just when to put all that respect to one side and give me exactly what I needed.

And I gave it right back to him, coming with him, feeling the wave of pleasure hit me one more time as he began to pump into me, or at least into the condom he had wrapped himself in, as always.

His movements gradually slowed, then stopped, as the frenzy that had consumed us both began to subside, and a moment later, he pulled out of me. With him no longer supporting me, my limbs gave way as I collapsed down onto the bed, resting my head against the pillow while he took the condom off and tossed it in the trash. The bed dipped beside me as he joined me on the bed, both of us staring up at the ceiling rather than at each other as we tried to process everything that had just happened.

For several minutes, neither of us spoke, as though we were afraid of breaking the spell that had descended on the room. That had been as close to perfect sex as I'd ever had, and I knew, I just *knew*, that whatever words were uttered next were going to change everything.

Sometimes, I really hated being right.

Cam spoke first, turning to me with a tentative smile. "Well, that was one hell of an apology."

I almost smiled back until I realized what he meant, and any hint of good humour fled my body as ice ran through my veins instead. "Wait. Do you think that was me *apologizing*?"

His brow furrowed in confusion, his brown eyes looking lost beneath his damp hair, beaded with sweat from the exertion of what we'd just done. "Wasn't it?"

He *had* to be kidding. "You really don't get it, do you?"

Why did I expect anything different? With frustration seething beneath my skin, I got to my feet and began to gather up my clothes while Cam sat up, watching me in bewilderment. "What are you doing?"

"What does it look like, Einstein? I'm going home. This was a mistake."

His jaw clenched, hard, as his nostrils flared. "Don't run away again, Tonia. We can't just pretend this never happened. This was something real."

"Really stupid." My hands trembled as I tried to rebutton my blouse. "Don't worry. I'm taking the blame for this one. I started it, and it was a stupid idea. I can own that."

"Can't we talk about this?" He made no move to stop me, staying on the bed, still naked as he made his appeal. Although he asked the question, it looked like he already knew what the answer would be and he was right.

"I don't think so." Patting my pockets, I double checked that I still had my keys and wallet. Luckily, I had dropped everything in one place on the floor when I stripped earlier, so nothing had fallen all out of place. I had everything I'd arrived with, except my self-respect. "I'll see you in the office tomorrow."

With that, I walked away, my emotions in even more turmoil than they had been when I got there. *So much for keeping things professional.*

~**Cam**~

The silence that descended over the room once Tonia shut the front door of my apartment behind her felt unbearably heavy, making it hard to breathe.

What the hell was that?

The best sex of my life, that much I knew, but beyond that, I didn't have a clue what to make of it. If I weren't completely naked and my cock still slightly sticky, I would have to wonder if I'd imagined the whole thing.

It came so completely out of the blue, like a shooting star lighting up the sky for one brief, shining moment, and now that it had gone, the world seemed a little bit darker, though in reality, it had just gone back to the way it was before.

At that moment, I only understood one thing for certain: I couldn't put myself through that again. I couldn't get my hopes up and imagine some kind of future with her only to have her walk away without a backward glance. It nearly broke me once before, and I didn't know if my heart would survive a second time.

"Remember, don't say anything to anyone about prom until I've talked about it with Tonia," I told Marley that morning, the morning it all fell apart, after I made sure she had breakfast and all her stuff for school. For the previous two weeks, I'd been looking after her during pretty much every spare minute I had, and I felt pretty sure that without me, she'd have been dead or in jail.

I hadn't told anyone about her situation, out of respect for her wishes, but I would have to tell Tonia that day. I would have to tell her everything.

Not saying anything to Tonia before then had been eating me up inside. I'd never kept a secret from her before, and I'd definitely never lied to her face, not like I did when she asked me if I knew Marley. She knew everything about me, every stupid, embarrassing thing I'd done or thought I ever had. I could trust her with anything, and though I'd tried to explain that to Marley, she just didn't see it. She thought telling Tonia would mean the whole world would know about it, and the thought nearly sent her into a panic.

I found myself torn between two promises: one to the girl I loved, to always be truthful with her, and the other to this girl I now felt responsible for, to keep her secret. Marley's mother was dying and her father had all but abandoned her. She was emotionally fragile and the stress seemed to be making her a little mentally unstable too. When I told her I couldn't take her to prom, she got so upset that I honestly feared she might do something extreme if I didn't agree. That fear had been the only reason I gave in, but the truth was that I had no intention of actually doing it.

Prom had been something Tonia and I looked forward to for years, and she deserved to have the night she'd dreamed of. If I could, I would make every one of her dreams come true. Seeing that beautiful smile and the trusting look in her deep blue eyes honestly meant the world to me, so when I told Marley I would take her, I lied, simple as that.

My actual plan for that morning was to talk to Tonia, to tell her everything, and to ask for her help. Together, we could find a way to get Marley to the prom and make sure she had a good time, something she could happily share with her mother. It would still be a good experience for her, just not with me.

Together, Tonia and I could do anything, and although I knew she'd be angry with me that I hadn't told her before, my prevailing feeling as I walked home in the early morning sunshine was one of relief. I couldn't wait to get it all out in the open and get rid of the gnawing feeling in my stomach that had been plaguing me ever since the day I caught Marley shoplifting in the store. After Tonia ranted and raved at me and called me an idiot, which she certainly would, then we could move on to solving the problem together, just as we always did.

For that reason, I'd told Marley not to say a word to anyone. I didn't want her to tell people she was going to prom with me and then have to take it back when it didn't happen. I didn't want her to lose face.

However, by the time I'd stopped off at home, gotten myself ready for the day, and made it to school, things had already gotten out of hand. Marley had blabbed, Tonia heard about it, and all hell broke loose.

I did end up taking Marley to prom, but only because Tonia broke up with me. It had been one of the most miserable nights of my life, but I suffered through it and took the pictures for Marley and her mom, only because Tonia broke my heart by believing that I would ever do that to her in the first place. She never even gave me a chance to explain, and after the shock had worn off, indignation took it place. Begging had never been in my DNA; if she wanted to know what happened and why I'd done it, she could come and apologize to me first.

After six long years, I thought she finally had.

So, in the delicate moment after we had sex, in the stillness of my bedroom with no sound but our heavy breathing as we both tried to find our equilibrium again, I tried to think of the right thing to say. A hundred different things were considered and rejected before I decided on the words that finally came out of my mouth.

"Well, that was one hell of an apology."

Admitting she'd made a mistake had never come easy to Tonia, so I didn't want it to make her uncomfortable. I thought by making light of it, by letting her know that I got the message even if she hadn't actually said the words out loud, it would help to keep her at ease.

Instead, she jumped up and ran out, claiming I'd missed the point and that it hadn't been an apology at all. Then what the hell was it? If she was still so angry with me, why did she have sex with me? She told me I didn't get it, and on that point, we were in complete agreement.

Just when I thought we might actually be able to move on, she yanked the rug back out from under me, and I couldn't keep giving her a chance to do it again. At some point, I had to accept that she and I were simply not meant to be.

I thought I had accepted it before, but the ease with which I fell right back into thinking about her, caring about her, and fucking her, made it clear I wasn't as over her as I thought.

I would have to try harder.

So, when she showed up at my office door at twenty minutes before nine the next morning, looking downright sinful in a red lacy top and a black-and-white checked skirt, her blonde hair pulled back in a professional bun, asking if we could talk before the work day started, I did the only thing I could: I turned her down.

"I don't think there's anything to talk about. You made things pretty clear last night, Sugar. We made a mistake."

Even repeating the word stung, but she'd called it exactly that. I was only following her script.

Tonia glanced over her shoulder before taking a few steps further into my office and lowering her voice. "Look, Cam, I know running out on you was childish. I was overwhelmed. I didn't expect that to happen when I came over, and I didn't expect... well, I didn't expect it to be like that. And then you brought the past back into it, and I just... I needed some time to process things."

It took fighting against every instinct I had to stick to my resolution to let go of the foolish hope that rose inside me, wondering what she might have decided, but in the end, I stuck to my guns. For my heart's sake, I had to.

"You leaving gave me some time to process things too. Seems to me we were both doing just fine for ourselves until we ended up working together. We said we'd keep it professional, and we've both failed: me by coming down to Corpus Christi last weekend and you by coming to my apartment last night. We're both to blame, but it doesn't mean we can't do better. We're capable of keeping this professional for the next two and a half weeks if we really try, so unless you're here to talk to me about business, then I respectfully decline the offer of a conversation."

Her lips set to a thin line as she stared at me from across my desk. "Don't be so stubborn, Bailey."

I had to laugh. "Is that really a word you should be throwing around at other people, Sugar?"

That only made her jaw clench harder before she muttered under her breath, "I should have known better." Turning on her heel, she headed out the door.

She'd summed it up precisely: I should have known better too. We both should have. Maybe one day, we finally would.

~**Tonia**~

My blood simmered just below the boiling point as I walked out of Cam's office and out of the office entirely. I needed some air.

Why did he always have to be so bullheaded? Always so damn sure that he was in the right, no matter what the situation.

I had actually shown up early that morning ready to admit I owed him an apology; not for six years ago, but for the night before. I shouldn't have left like I did, but at the moment, it really felt like the only option. How was I supposed to talk to him about what happened and what I felt if I didn't understand it myself?

Did what Marley told me change what happened all those years ago? The answer to that couldn't be easily pinned down. The answer included both yes and no.

It meant a lot to know he hadn't been cheating on me. I had never been able to fully reconcile that with the boy I loved, so I was relieved to know my judgement hadn't been that flawed. On top of that, I could respect what he'd been doing for Marley. Not many people would have done the same, and to do it for someone he didn't even really know before it all started was just one more example of what made him such a good, decent human being.

But why didn't he trust me enough to tell me the truth? And more than that, once he knew what I thought had happened, why didn't he ever correct me? Why did he let me believe the worst of him, and let me believe I was the kind of girl that a kind of guy like him would cheat on?

Why didn't he fight for me? Why didn't he fight for *us?*

I walked away because I thought we had nothing left worth fighting for, but he knew otherwise, and he just let me go anyway.

Those were the questions I wanted answered in his office that morning, but, as usual with Cam, it had to be his way or no way at all. Since I didn't want to talk last night, he didn't want to talk now. It infuriated me. *He* infuriated me.

Even if he had grown into a ridiculously good-looking sex god.

With that frustrating thought in my head, I yanked the main door of the office open just as Jason's assistant Marianne swiped her card on the other side, and she jumped back in alarm.

"Sorry," I apologized abruptly. "I'm just heading out for coffee."

Still blinking in surprise, she called out after me as I started down the hall. "Wait, Tonia, do you mind if I tag along? I kind of wanted to ask you about something."

Every nerve in my body screamed that I wanted to be left alone, but I pushed down that response. Telling her I had really just been about to go and scream down an empty alleyway in frustration would make me sound a little crazy.

Marianne and I had spoken a few times since I'd started at Barnly Oil, but only in passing. If she wanted to talk to me, I should take advantage of the opportunity. My job there was to help and impress people, and I couldn't let Cameron Bailey throw me off my game.

"Of course," I told her, as though that had been my intention all along. "I'd love the company."

Her face relaxed into a warm smile. "Wonderful. Let me just drop these files at my desk."

She stepped into the office to do that, returning to me a minute later. Together, we took the elevator downstairs and exited the building, making small talk as we stepped into the morning sunshine. The air felt fresh and the sun warm on my skin as I did my best to put my frustration behind me.

"I hope it's not out of line," she said as we walked side-by-side down the sidewalk. "But there aren't a lot of other women in the office for me to talk to, and you just seem so... together, you know?"

I had to stifle a laugh. If she only knew how not-together I felt at that moment, she'd feel pretty foolish for saying so.

"Is someone in the office giving you trouble?" I tried to guess. She had mentioned on my first day that the men were all more respectful than she'd expected, but after my own experience with Bradyn, I wouldn't be shocked to find out something had happened.

She quickly shook her head. "No, nothing like that. It's just... I think I'm falling for someone, and I don't know what to do. Is that really wrong? How bad is it?"

"Someone in the office, you mean?" It felt like she meant that, but I didn't want to jump to any conclusions.

Her nod let me know I had it absolutely right. "Sometimes, I think he likes me too, but he hasn't said anything."

Thinking back to my lunch with Jason on Monday, I had to grimace. "Well, it can be tricky, and the last thing you want to do is put yourself out there if they don't feel the same, and then you still have to work together every day."

Marianne nodded again, more emphatically. "That's exactly what I'm afraid of. What should I do?"

We arrived at the coffee shop and went in to place our orders, giving me time to think over my response. There was no blanket answer for that kind of situation, and I could hardly claim to be an expert on relationships, especially workplace ones, but I would do my best to give her some things to think about at least.

"Well, the chances are that if he *is* interested, he's not going to make a move in the office," I told her as we sat down at a nearby table. After all, I never would have said anything to Jason at the office; I'd waited until we were out for lunch before I brought it up. "Is there any way you could spend time with him outside of work?"

Her eyes lit up as she took a sip from her take-out coffee cup, leaving a perfect red lip imprint on the cardboard rim. "Actually, a whole bunch of people are going out for drinks after work tomorrow, and I'm pretty sure he'll be there. I wasn't sure if I should go since I'm just an assistant."

"You definitely should go," I assured her. "Leaving aside any possible flirtation that might take place, you have every right to be there. You're just as much a part of this company as anyone else, even the CEO."

Her cheeks flushed as she looked down at her coffee cup, and suddenly, I put it all together.

"Wait, is it Jason that we're talking about?"

Her eyes snapped up to me in dismay. "Oh my gosh, am I that obvious?"

"No, not at all," I assured her, only lying a little bit as my mind raced. Cam had said Jason was interested in someone in the office; could he have been talking about Marianne? It seemed possible, but unlike Cam, I had no intention of opening my mouth without being certain of it.

What I could do, however, was give her a little nudge in the right direction.

"He definitely seems like he wants to foster an inclusive working environment, so I'm sure he'd be more than happy if you went. Don't try too hard, just have a good time on your own, and if he wants to seek you out, he will."

She nodded as she thought that over before giving me a hopeful smile. "Would you come along too? I'd feel better if you were there to make sure I don't do anything stupid."

I had walked right into that one, hadn't I? After the last few days, going out for drinks with Cam, even surrounded by other people, seemed like a terrible idea, but the pleading look that Marianne gave me was hard to resist.

"I'll have to check my calendar," I tried to demur, but as her face fell, I gave in. "But I'm pretty sure I'm free."

If that kept up, I would soon be as much of a soft touch as Cam, but I tried to tell myself it would be fine. After all, how much worse could things get?

Chapter Nine

~Cam~

By the time Tonia returned to my office for our appointment that afternoon, she looked calm, cool and composed, and I did my best to match her. We stuck to business, neither of us alluding in any way to either the past or what happened the night before. From the outside, no one would have had a clue that we were anything more than business acquaintances.

Inside was a different matter. Inside, I couldn't stop thinking about the way it felt to be with her again.

Her legs crossed as she adjusted on her chair, and I could almost feel those legs wrapped around me. A whiff of her perfume hit me as she leaned over to show me something on the screen, and I remembered the way it lingered in my room after she'd gone. She tucked a loose strand of hair behind her ear, and I could hear the words I'd whispered to her the night before, the dirty words spoken directly against her skin.

Did I affect her the same way? Was she thinking about it too? Or was she really just as focused on work as she appeared to be?

When our time had finished, Tonia got to her feet and packed up her things, keeping her eyes on her bag as she spoke. "I've been invited to go out for drinks after work tomorrow with some other people from the office. I'm not sure if you were planning on going, but if it's going to be a problem, I can make an excuse. This is your workplace, after all."

Though I appreciated the consideration, I didn't think avoiding each other was necessary. "For this month, it's your workplace too. Don't let me stop you from doing anything you'd normally do."

Her response to that was a curt nod. "Alright. See you tomorrow, then."

"See you tomorrow."

When she had gone, I exhaled, perhaps in relief or perhaps in disappointment, which would be ridiculous. She'd done just what I asked in keeping things professional, so I had no earthly reason to be disappointed.

Sighing at myself and my contradictory emotions, I did my best to put it all out of my mind. I almost succeeded too, until I got home after work and found Marley waiting for me outside the door of my apartment building.

"Oh, come on," I muttered under my breath. Why did the universe have it in for me? Normally, I wouldn't mind talking to Marley, but she had probably shown up to apologize for telling Tonia what happened even after she swore she wouldn't, and I really didn't have it in me to rehash everything one more time. I had been planning on going to the gym and running on the treadmill until my lungs burned and I felt nothing except the pain in my muscles. It would be better than the dumpster fire inside my head.

"Tonia already told you, didn't she?" Marley guessed as I walked up to where she stood. The way she twisted her hands nervously made her look a lot like the 16-year-old girl I'd known all those years ago.

"Of course she did," I answered bluntly. "Did you think she wouldn't?"

"No," she admitted with a wince. "I always knew she was the kind of person who wouldn't keep a secret."

That stung, as she must have known it would. All those years, she insisted I'd done the right thing by keeping the truth from Tonia because

Tonia would never have kept it to herself. In Marley's eyes, she'd just been proven right.

"It's not the same thing," was all I said in response. "What brings you to town, anyway?"

"I'm here to check on my dad." Marley's dad had never fully recovered from the loss of his wife, and he'd never returned to Sandy Creek either. When word got out in town that Marley's mother had died, other people from the church offered to take her in so she wouldn't have to change schools. By the time I left for college, she had moved in with a family who had a teenage daughter of their own, and she and Marley became close friends.

Other than her mother dying, things had worked out pretty well for Marley, all things considered.

"Can I join you for dinner?" she asked me with a tentative smile. "My treat."

Against my better judgement, I agreed. Partly, I just didn't have the will to argue, and part of me was curious about exactly what she'd said to Tonia, even though it absolutely should not matter to me. "You don't need to buy me dinner. I've got some steaks upstairs, come on."

Marley had been to my apartment once before, the last time she was in town, so she made herself at home, fixing a salad while I quickly grilled the steaks. Not being allowed to have a proper barbecue was really my only complaint about living in an apartment building. Otherwise, it suited me just fine.

Sitting down with the steak, salad and a beer at the table on my balcony, Marley launched into her explanation, telling me exactly what she'd said to Tonia. None of it surprised me; she'd told her the whole story as far as she knew it.

"I knew after we talked last week that you were all worked up about Tonia again, and then I heard that you were at the hospital with her over the weekend."

I almost had my mouth open to ask where she heard that until I remembered the Sandy Creek rumour mill and closed it again. Dumb question.

"I just thought it would be better to get it all out in the open, finally, and you could finally know for sure if you two have any chance of getting back together."

Did I want that? Had I secretly been hoping for it all these years? I hadn't thought so, but after what happened the night before, I couldn't really deny it either. Somewhere deep inside, I must have had a secret fantasy that when Tonia knew the truth, she would admit she'd been wrong not to trust me, and she'd want to pick up right where we left off.

In one way, that had come true with our fantastic sex, but in the deeper, more important way, it hadn't, and it looked like I would have to accept that it never would. Maybe that explained why her walking out last night hurt so much: it meant I finally had to put that dream to rest, once and for all.

I answered Marley as succinctly as I could. "Well, I appreciate the effort, but it looks like that ship has sailed. It just wasn't meant to be, I guess."

"At least now you know," she replied sympathetically, shuffling her seat a little closer to mine. "And you can finally move on."

"I have moved on," I protested. "I'd dated a lot of other women."

"And how long was your longest relationship?" she pressed.

The question made me wince. She knew how to go for the jugular. "A couple of months, I guess."

It never seemed to work out. Things were fine as long as we were keeping things light and having a good time. When we tried to move on to the next level, my heart was never quite in it, and the women could tell.

"Because you weren't completely over Tonia, no matter what you thought," Marley suggested. "But now, you've finally got closure. Now, you know."

And with that, she leaned over and kissed me.

My mind and body both froze momentarily for just a moment before I placed my hands on her shoulders and pushed her firmly back. "What are you doing?"

We didn't have that kind of relationship. We never had. I thought of her as a friend, or even a little sister in some ways, but definitely not as someone that I wanted to kiss. Not ever, really, but especially not after the emotional turmoil of the last week and the incredible night I'd just spent with Tonia.

Several different emotions flashed across Marley's face, everything from hurt to confusion to embarrassment. "But I thought..."

"What did you think?" I honestly had no idea where this was coming from as I pushed my chair back, putting more space between us, and her face fell even further.

She looked away from me, and for a moment, I thought she might refuse to answer, or even run away like Tonia did when things got overwhelming. But after thinking about it for a minute, she turned back to me with a look of determination.

"I thought you just needed to get over her. I've watched you struggle to be happy, but I thought you would get there once you just let it go. I never thought it would take so long. And I thought... well, I thought that when you finally did, you'd give us another chance. After all, you chose me over her once before."

What in the world was she talking about? "I never chose you over Tonia."

Her look of certainty melded into confusion again. "You took me to prom instead of her."

She really thought that was a choice? "Because she broke up with me. Because she got suspended and banned from going. Because your mother was dying."

She winced at the last one, but I didn't regret saying it. Every word was true, and Marley might be right about one thing: the time had come to lay it all on the table, once and for all.

"But you were going to take me even before she broke up with you," she reminded me, and once more, I didn't hold back.

I never intended to tell her I'd lied about that, not after the way everything played out, but somewhere along the way, a wire had gotten crossed. If she had really spent all these years hoping to rekindle something that never existed in the first place, it would be kinder to tell her the truth, even if it hurt in the short term. "Marley, I only said that because you threatened to kill yourself if I didn't."

Her face went pale as she blinked at me in disbelief. When she spoke again, the words were hardly a whisper. "I never said that."

"Not in those words," I admitted. "But what was I supposed to think? I told you I couldn't take you, and you started crying and talking about how you wished you were the one dying rather than your mother. That terrified me. I didn't know what to do. I was just a kid too, and I was only trying to help. So I said I would take you, but it never for a moment meant that I chose you over Tonia."

Her lower lip began to wobble as she thought it over. "So, you never wanted to go with me? Not even a little bit?"

Taking a deep breath, I tried to tell her the truth as calmly and gently as I could. "Marley, I never thought of you as anything other than a friend, and to be totally honest, I never intended to take you to prom even though I said I would. I planned to tell Tonia everything that morning and ask for her help. I thought you needed a counsellor, not a prom date."

Even though I tried to soften the blow, the words still hit her hard. It was almost crazy how strong our emotions still were over things that happened years ago; not just Marley's, but Tonia's and mine as well. I supposed some things glanced off us, but others sunk beneath the skin, burying in deep, and this was one of those things. It had changed my life and Tonia's, and now, I began to see just how much it affected Marley too.

I honestly never had any idea she had hopes of us being together, not then, and especially not now.

"So, all this time, you've just felt sorry for me."

Her voice sounded flat and distant, but what she said wasn't the truth either, and despite everything, I didn't want her to think it was. "At the time, that accounted for most of it. Since then, over the past six years, I've gotten to know you better and I *do* like you, as a friend. But only ever as a friend, Marley. What I felt for Tonia was completely different."

She still looked confused. "Then why did you take me to the prom in the end?"

"Because I'd already lost my girlfriend over it. It seemed stupid not to have something good come out of it in the end. At least you got the pictures to take to your mom."

Marley had told me just how happy those photos had made her mother, the last time they saw each other. She died the following week.

Her getting to see those photos before she passed had been the one good thing to come out of the whole sorry mess.

"But did you really think I had a good time that night?" I asked her next.

My memories of that night mostly involved half the school avoiding me because they thought, like Tonia did, that I'd cheated on her, or making fun of me for being there with Marley in the first place. Nothing about that night counted as a happy memory for me. I spent the whole end of our senior year being miserable.

"I knew you were upset about Tonia," she admitted. "But I thought you just needed time. I thought you'd go away to college and get over it. I thought for sure once you got a job and got your life started here that you'd get over it, but you never have."

"I *am* over it," I argued. "Me not wanting a relationship with you has nothing to do with Tonia."

"Maybe not, but you not wanting a relationship with anyone is a different story. You might think I'm a bitch for telling her the truth yesterday, but honestly, I did it for you. And yes, before you say anything, maybe part of it was for me too, but as much as I hoped you might want to move on with me, mostly I just want to see you move on. It's been six years. You deserve to be happy, and Tonia isn't the one who can give you that. You need to let her go, for real this time."

I thought I had. I had certainly tried.

Maybe I just didn't know how.

"I should go." Marley stood up and grabbed the empty plates off the table. "I'm sorry for tonight."

Standing up myself, I followed her back into the kitchen. "Is this why you haven't found someone yourself? Were you waiting on me?"

She winced one last time. "I don't know. Maybe?"

What was wrong with the both of us? We made a sorry pair, and despite the awkwardness, I hoped this talk had done us good. Maybe now that the truth was out there, we could all put this behind us, not just me and Marley, but Tonia too. Maybe this would be the final nudge I needed to let go of Tonia at last.

I kept thinking about it after Marley left, and the more I thought about it, the more convinced I became about what I needed to do. The time had never been better to make a fresh start, and there was no time like the present. The next night, when we all went out for drinks after work, I would show Tonia exactly how over her I was.

~**Tonia**~

I didn't give myself time to brood when I got home from work on Wednesday. First, I made a few calls to make sure everything was in place for the get-together at Dex's new gallery on Friday. He'd only asked me to arrange some food, but I wanted to do more than that. We were celebrating Dex's achievement, certainly, but we were also celebrating Shawna for being a fighter and making it through another initial round of chemo. With that in mind, I organized some balloons and flowers and cake along with supper. I even bought some art supplies so that we could all take part in creating something to mark the occasion without using up Dex's own supplies.

Maybe it would be over-the-top, but I didn't care. Life had enough crappy moments to deal with, so when a good thing came along, we might as well make a fuss about it.

And speaking of dealing with the less-good things, I also did some prep work for the following night's after-work drinks. Putting me and Cam and booze in the same room seemed like a recipe for disaster, so I didn't intend to let it get out of control. If I couldn't control myself on my own, I would need to bring in some backup.

I didn't have an appointment with Cam in the office on Thursday, splitting my time between two of the other executives, and I did my best not to look when I heard his laugh or his rumbling voice as he spoke to some of the other people in the office.

If I let myself, it would be all too easy to remember that voice in my ear when we were in his apartment the other night. In fact, goosebumps erupted down my arms even as I tried not to think about it. It wouldn't take long to move from that to remembering the feel of his lips on my skin or the look of hunger in his eyes, and soon my whole body ached with longing, which was hardly what I needed in the middle of a training session.

When the work day ended, Marianne and I and some of the other women in the office took a trip to the restroom, doing some last-minute primping before we headed out. The room was filled with laughter, but I could sense some nerves too. The company was still young, this evening would be one of their first social events, and there were a lot of young, single people of both genders. The possibility for flirtation and maybe even the odd hook-up or two ran high.

"Have you got your eye on anyone tonight, Tonia?" one of the account managers asked me as I touched up my makeup. "You've spent a lot of one-on-one time with most of the senior managers."

She sounded rather jealous of that fact, and a quick glance around the room showed me all the other women were listening curiously to see what my response would be.

I quickly set their minds at ease. "Not at all. In fact, I've got someone coming to meet me at the bar."

That seemed to take the woman by surprise. "Really? I could have sworn you and Bradyn had some chemistry going on. Didn't you spend some time together down in Corpus Christi?"

It took all my self-control not to choke on my response. "Not that kind of time. If you're interested in Bradyn, you don't have to worry about me."

"I thought you and Cameron had something," one of the other ones piped up. "He can't take his eyes off you, I've noticed."

I tried not to flush at that idea, but someone else quickly jumped in so luckily, I didn't have to answer. "And I thought you were into Jason. You've had a couple of lunches with him."

Marianne looked taken aback by that, so I quickly tried to reassure her and put all the rumours to rest at once. "I'm not into *anyone* here. I'm just here to do my job and at the end of the month, I'll be gone. I had no idea you were all paying so much attention."

That made them laugh, as I'd hoped. "We need something fun to talk about when the men all start on their fantasy football league," the first one told me, and thankfully, with that comment, they moved on to other topics.

"Did you really invite a guy tonight?" Marianne whispered to me as we made our way outside.

"I did, but don't worry. I'm still there to be your wingwoman."

She gave me a grateful smile, despite being completely in the dark about the real reason I'd invited Tyler. He and I dated for a while a couple of years ago. Our breakup had been amicable and we were still in touch; we still liked each other, we'd just realized we wanted different things in the long term. As I liked to put it: he wanted a wife who would cater to his every whim, and I wanted some dignity. Of course, the truth wasn't quite so black and white.

In any case, we were still friends, and when I decided I wanted a buffer that night, he was the first person who came to mind.

"I'm going to finally get to meet the famous Cam?" he asked, sounding intrigued when I called him. "I thought you might have made him up. I wasn't entirely sure someone so purely evil actually existed."

"He's real all right, but I don't think I ever said he was evil." At least, I didn't think I had. "Anyway, you don't need to talk to him. Just sit next to me and make sure I don't do anything stupid."

He let out a loud laugh. "If I'd been any good at doing that, we wouldn't have broken up. You said you'd pay for drinks, though, so I'll be there."

Several of the men from the office were waiting for us in the lobby and we all walked over to the bar together. Cam wasn't in the group and neither was Jason. Perhaps they'd got caught up in something, or perhaps Cam had merely decided to avoid me. I couldn't guess which seemed more likely.

To my relief, Tyler had already arrived at the bar by the time we got there, and I quickly introduced him to everyone. Several of the women gave him appreciative looks, so maybe he'd pick up a number or two to make the evening worth his time once I made it clear there was nothing between us. For the time being, though, I sat next to him, looking to all the world like we were a couple as we headed to the area reserved for our party. There were two tall tables with stools and a handful of armchairs around a coffee table next to it. We all claimed tall tables, the women jockeying to find the spot that would let them show themselves off to their best advantage.

About twenty minutes later, Tyler leaned closer to me. "I don't want to jump to conclusions but I'm guessing that's Cam who just walked in."

I fought the urge to look over at the door for myself. "Why do you say that?"

"Because he's looking at us like he just swallowed a lemon."

With that mental image, I couldn't stop myself from glancing over, and sure enough, Cam stood just inside the door, looking our way with a rather sour expression on his face. As soon as he saw me looking, he immediately turned away.

Good. That should keep him away from me for the evening, just like I planned. He and Jason came over to where our group sat, taking spots about as far away from me as possible.

I didn't plan on the blonde woman who walked up to him just a few minutes later, however. "This is Kyra," I heard him say to the group at large. "She lives in my building."

It appeared he'd had the same idea I did. I knew for a fact he wasn't dating anyone, so he must have brought her along simply to keep me at arm's length.

"You doing okay there, Tonia?" Tyler gave me a far-too-knowing smirk. "It looks like you just had a taste of whatever he was drinking earlier. Looks like you're both playing the same game, trying to make each other jealous."

"I'm not trying to make him jealous," I protested.

"Well, maybe you should be, because it sure looks like that's his plan."

Again, even though I didn't want to, I couldn't help looking to see what he meant. With no room at the tall tables, Cam had taken a seat on one of the armchairs and Kyra had perched herself on the arm of his chair. With his arm around her waist, she giggled at something he'd said like she'd never heard anything funnier.

It didn't matter to me, I reminded myself. He could be there with whomever he wanted. He made it perfectly clear to me the day before that he wanted to forget all about what happened between us. He wouldn't even talk about it.

So surely, it wouldn't bother him that I had brought someone else along that night.

Would it?

"You think you'd be able to pull that off?" I asked Tyler, simply out of curiosity. I didn't actually intend to do anything so childish.

He grinned before leaning over to whisper directly in my ear. "I'll take it as a personal insult if he's not threatening to fight me by the end of the night, especially since he's already looking over at us right now. The only question is, how far do you want to push him?"

~Cam~

It took me a moment to realize the woman beside me had said my name, trying to get my attention.

"Cam?"

Blinking, I quickly turned my head away from where Tonia and the overly attentive man next to her were whispering, and looked up at Kyra hovering over me. "Sorry, what was that?"

"I asked if you want a drink." Her smile had turned slightly wary as she glanced over in the direction I'd just been looking. "Is everything okay?"

Everything was *not* okay, to my great frustration. I shouldn't care that Tonia had brought someone else with her. He must have come with her, because he definitely wasn't from the office, and they certainly seemed to know each other. I had just told Marley the night before that I was over Tonia, and for that reason, I had brought my own guest tonight. Kyra was one of the women who worked out in the gym in my building, one who often flirted with me but I'd never encouraged before, and when I saw her in the gym that morning, I asked her if she wanted to join me for drinks tonight. I made it clear it would only be as friends, but she had been happy to come along anyway.

Making Tonia jealous wasn't my aim, since she hadn't given me any indication that she would care. After all, she had seen me with another woman the night she showed up at my apartment building, and it didn't seem to bother her, or to stop her from inviting herself up to my apartment. Rather than being provocative, I simply wanted to show her I wasn't fixating on her or what happened between us earlier that week.

But if I *was* over her, as I said I was, then why did the sight of her with another man make me want to scratch my skin off?

"I'm fine," I lied to Kyra, trying to smile even though it felt wrong. "I'll get the drinks though, you stay put. What would you like?"

She gave me her order, some fruity cocktail I'd never heard of before, and I headed up to the bar, passing along the info to the bartender and doing my best not to turn around and check on Tonia and her companion while I waited.

I managed to pull it off too, at least until the guy in question sidled up to the bar next to me. "Two Lone Stars," he told the bartender before glancing over at me. "Hey, you're with this Barnly group, right? I'm Tyler, I'm a friend of Tonia Callahan."

He offered his hand and I had no choice but to shake it. "Cam."

"Nice to meet you. What do you do at the company, Cam?"

We made small talk about my job while his beers and mine were brought over. I still had to wait on Kyra's drink, and Tyler didn't seem to be in a hurry to get back, so I asked the burning question in my mind, as casually as possible while taking a swig of my drink. "So, you're here with Tonia? How do you guys know each other?"

"We dated for a while at the end of college," he told me, and it took all my self-control not to spit out the mouthful of beer I'd just taken. "Didn't work out then, but we just got back in touch, and I'm feeling pretty good about it. I always kind of felt she was the one that got away, you know?"

I certainly did know. There was very little that I knew about better than that.

"Better to regret the things you did than the ones you didn't, isn't that what people say?" Tyler continued, raising his beer in a toast. "Here's to taking a shot."

With that, he headed back to the table, handing the other beer to Tonia and leaning over to whisper in her ear again, his hand resting on her arm.

"Sir? Your drink?"

Once again, I hadn't realized I was staring until the bartender tried to get my attention.

"Thanks," I mumbled as I took it from him and headed back over to my own table.

Kyra gave me a smile as she took her drink from me. She clicked it against my beer bottle, and we both took a drink as Bradyn nodded his head at me. "We were just talking about first kisses, Cam. Time for your story."

For the second time in a matter of minutes, I nearly spit out my beer. "How the hell did that come up?"

"My nephew asked me for advice," Jason explained. "So, we were just seeing who had the worst experience and so far, Bradyn's winning for kissing what he thought was his sister's friend, but was actually her friend's brother."

Everyone laughed, clearly having enjoyed the story the first time around.

"Can you beat that?" Jason asked, leaning forward in anticipation.

In an attempt to keep my eyes from wandering over to Tonia, I looked at Kyra instead, who smiled at me, waiting eagerly for my story as well.

"I hate to disappoint y'all, but my first kiss was pretty dang wonderful."

They all groaned in disappointment, except for Kyra, who looked intrigued. "What made it good? Did you have it all planned in advance?"

The memories came back to me whether I wanted them to or not, of Tonia and I out on a dirt road outside Sandy Creek. We'd biked out to the fishing pond just out of town, and on the way back, I skidded on some loose gravel and wiped out. I was 14 years old and desperate not to cry in front of the girl I'd had a crush on for years. She pulled some pink Band-Aids out of her bag, and though she tried to be gentle, it still stung. A tear slipped down my cheek before I could hide it, but Tonia didn't care. She reached over and wiped it away, and as soon as her hand touched my face, I couldn't help myself. My hands went to her face too, and I kissed her, down on the ground on that dirt road, blood on my fingertips and hers, the sun setting behind us and flies buzzing around us, and neither of us having the first idea what we were supposed to do.

It was absolutely perfect.

"I didn't plan it at all," I told Kyra. "The girl involved made it special."

Several of the guys made gagging sounds as Bradyn coughed "bullshit" into his hand. They moved on to the next guy, but Kyra seemed to appreciate my answer, giving me a warm smile.

"That's sweet." Her hand went to my thigh as she leaned closer to me. "And I'm sure you've improved since then."

The invitation in her words came through loud and clear, but my thoughts were still on Tonia, and I couldn't stop myself from looking over at her, just in time to catch her looking in my direction. As soon as our eyes connected, she turned her head, laughing at something Tyler had said. She leaned a bit closer to him, his arm went around her, and my stomach turned.

This was ridiculous.

I needed a break. Placing my beer down on the table, I got to my feet. "I'll be right back," I told my guest before heading off in search of the restrooms. They were individual ones, a set of four doors down a narrow hallway, and I went into the last one, locking the door behind me and staring at my reflection in the mirror. The guy I saw there looked pretty pathetically miserable.

Obviously, my plan wasn't working. I'd tried ignoring her. I'd tried being professional with her. We'd had that spectacular night together, which should have satisfied any lingering curiosity. If I was really over her, this shouldn't be so hard.

The only conclusion that made any sense, then, was that I *wasn't* over her. And if I still hadn't moved on, after all that time, would I ever be able to? Would there ever be a time when I didn't miss her or want her, even when she drove me up the wall?

The man in the mirror had no answers for me, and as I looked into his troubled eyes, I just wanted to go home. I thought I could handle tonight, I thought having Kyra there would help, but obviously, it didn't. I needed some space to think everything through and decide what the hell to do next, because everything I'd done to that point hadn't worked.

With that plan in mind, I yanked the door open, ready to head back out and make my excuses, but when the door opened, Tonia stood on the other side, waiting for me.

Before I could react, she pushed me back into the restroom, the combined mass and heat of our bodies making the small space even smaller, and she locked the door behind her.

"What are you..." I started to ask, but I didn't get a chance to finish my sentence before her lips pressed firmly and hungrily against mine.

Chapter Ten

~Tonia~

Cam's immediate, instinctive response when I kissed him was to kiss me back. Before his brain could kick in, before he could put his walls up, before he could think of all the reasons we shouldn't do this or couldn't do this, he simply kissed me back, and in doing so, answered the question I most wanted the answer to.

The signals he had been sending me that night were utterly baffling. He brought another woman with him, a woman who obviously wanted him, and he told me he didn't want to talk about what happened between us. Those were the signs of someone who wanted to cut ties and move on.

On the other hand, Tyler had a different opinion when he got back from the bar. "When I said I wanted to get back together with you, he squeezed that bottle of beer in his hand so tight, I thought it would break right there and then. If that guy's over you, I'm the next president of the United States."

At that point, Cam came back to his seat and I heard the other guys ask him about his first kiss. He didn't look at me, didn't acknowledge me in any way, but I heard his response anyway: "Pretty dang wonderful."

I felt just the same about it. No matter what had happened since then, there was no denying how wonderful that moment had been. It seemed time hadn't soured it for him either, which made me even more confused about why he insisted we had nothing to talk about. Those were all signs of someone who wasn't over much of anything at all.

So, when I followed him to the restroom, when I pushed him back inside where no one could see us and kissed him, a much harder and more experienced kiss than that first one he'd just been talking about, I simply wanted to see how he'd react. I wanted to know if he was hiding in there because he felt just as confused and conflicted as I did.

And I got my answer. His hands went to my waist, pulling me tight to him and his lips moved against mine with an intensity that stole my breath away. Heat raced through my body, spurred on by both his actions now and the memories of the night we shared together just a couple of days earlier.

Just as I could start to feel him hardening against me, Cam pulled back, taking a step back so quickly, he nearly tripped over the toilet, and stared at me in bewilderment. "What are we doing?"

Now he wanted to talk. Typical. "You didn't want to talk about it this morning," I reminded him. "And I don't want to talk right now. That's not why I'm here."

Having any kind of conversation was definitely not what I had in mind, not when my body ached for more.

His lips pressed together as he thought about it, but it didn't take him very long. In a matter of seconds, his arms were back around me and his mouth devouring mine once again.

Things had definitely changed since he was that kid with skinned knees on the dirt road outside of town. Then, his kiss had been tentative and unsure. There in the bar restroom, he knew exactly what to do, and he did it with no hesitation at all. His fingers ran through my hair, tugging just hard enough, just as I liked it, while the confident thrust of his tongue set my pulse racing. His hips angled against mine perfectly, letting me feel every concealed inch of him, hard and hot and ready.

"Do you have a condom?" I asked breathlessly. I knew without asking that he wouldn't do anything without one.

When he shook his head no, I felt both disappointed and strangely relieved. At least I knew he hadn't been expecting anything tonight with Kyra. His eyebrows raised as his lips spread into a smirk. "I don't carry a supply around in my pockets anymore, Sugar."

I had to laugh. He had indeed made a habit of carrying them around when we first started sleeping together, so that we were never caught out if our need for each other got too great, and I could remember him being mortified when he accidentally pulled one out in front of my dad while reaching into his pocket for something else.

Luckily, my dad had a sense of humour about it, but Cam couldn't look him in the eye for a week afterwards.

"I guess we'll just have to pretend we're in my parent's basement again, then," I whispered against his ear, my breath as hot as my body felt, and Cam groaned in approval, knowing exactly what I meant.

Back in those early days, when we were desperate for each other but getting naked was too risky, we simply got each other off, our hands down the other one's pants. A little mutual masturbation always worked to relieve the pressure.

His zipper got pulled down before I could get another word out, making me laugh again as he exhaled in relief. I'd worn a skirt that night, which made things easier for him, and when his fingers made contact with my damp panties, he groaned again.

"Fuck, Sugar, you're so wet."

He had that right, and it was all his damn fault.

I spit into my hand, getting a good amount of lubricant to start rubbing him with, my hand gripping his hard shaft firmly as his fingers slid beneath the fabric between my legs, brushing up against my clit.

"Oh, God," I muttered as he kissed my neck, one hand between my legs and the other on my breast. It was hard to keep focus on what I was meant to be doing, but I tried my best, pumping his stiff cock and twisting my hand gently around his head, making his muscles tighten.

"You've been thinking about my cock since the other night, haven't you?" he growled, his voice taking on that harder, slightly more dominant edge it always did when he got really turned on. "You've been thinking about it just as much as I've been missing this pussy."

He shoved his fingers deep into me as I swayed against him, supporting myself with one arm on his shoulder while my right hand continued to stroke him.

"Tyler couldn't get you off this quickly, could he?" Cam challenged, the jealousy and possessiveness in his voice completely clear. "He wasn't the one who got you wet like this."

He had that right, but I wasn't about to let him have the last word. "It's not Kyra's hand you want circling your cock, is it?"

"Fuck, no."

His simple admission of that fact brought me even closer, and he knew it, beginning to fuck me harder with his fingers, his thumb playing with my clit, and his own breath growing shorter as I picked up my pace in return.

"Give it to me, Sugar," he ordered, his voice thick with need. "Come all over my hand, sweet girl."

He hadn't called me that in a very long time, and my body obeyed, clamping down on his hand as my orgasm hit me, and that proved to be his tipping point too. He came hard, spurting all over my exposed thighs as I kept stroking him lightly.

As we both caught our breath, I looked down at the mess we'd made. "Well, shit."

He chuckled too, but only for a second before someone knocked on the door. "Cam? Is everything okay in there?"

The voice on the other side of the door belonged to Kyra, and it only made me smile wider as Cam's eyes widened like a deer caught in the headlights. How, exactly, did he plan to explain this?

~Cam~

I had no idea why Tonia found it funny that Kyra was outside the restroom door. When that door opened, she would be exposed just the same as me. Surely, her date wouldn't exactly be thrilled about what she'd just done either, not to mention the man who'd hired us both.

"Do up your pants," she whispered to me, still smirking. "I'll clean up the floor."

Since all she had to do was pull her skirt back down, she was a step ahead of me, and I moved out of the way while she took care of the mess we'd made

"I'll be just a second," I called out to Kyra as I tucked my cock back into my pants, zipped them up and quickly washed my hands. How long had I been away for her to come looking for me? What if I'd just been having stomach trouble? It felt like a pretty ballsy move, but as I glanced at my watch, I realized it had actually been over 20 minutes since I left the table. Maybe she had a valid reason for being concerned.

"Go ahead," Tonia whispered to me, still smiling. "I'll stay out of sight."

I didn't really want to go, not after what we'd just done. I still didn't have the first idea why she had come in there at all. Did she think we'd moved into some kind of friends with benefits situation? That would only make sense if we were actually friends in the first place, which I couldn't swear we were.

Did she just want a fuck buddy? As much as I enjoyed being intimate with her, I couldn't do that in the long term. I was supposed to be moving on, and being reminded of just how good we could have been together was hardly the way to do that. The pull between me and Tonia wasn't just about sex for me. It never had been.

Or had she come in there simply to convince me that we still had things to talk about?

Whatever her reason, I had no time to get an answer right then and there, so reluctantly, I opened the door while Tonia squeezed up against the wall behind it. It might not have been perfect, but I could manage to get out of the restroom without it being completely obvious that someone else had been in there with me.

"I'm so sorry, I lost track of time," I apologized to Kyra as I pulled the restroom door closed behind me. "Started checking something on my work phone, and got caught up on it. I didn't realize it had been so long."

As we started walking back down the hall, the restroom door clicked locked behind us. Kyra turned her head to look, so I quickly tried to distract her, putting my arm around her.

"Can I get you another drink?"

Her eyes were full of suspicion, letting me know she didn't really buy my story, and I couldn't really blame her. Calling it weak would be generous.

"I think I'd just like to go home, actually," she answered me coolly.

Some guys in my position would have told her to go ahead then, but unfortunately, that wasn't me. My conscience wouldn't allow it, not when I'd invited her there, even though I would much rather stay and talk to Tonia and figure out what the hell was going on in her head.

Maybe I could take Kyra home and come back before Tonia left for the night. My apartment building wasn't all that far away.

Since Tonia hadn't come back from the restroom yet, I went to talk to Tyler while Kyra collected her coat. "I've got to head out, but can you let Tonia know I'll be back later? There's something I want to talk to her about."

"Sure thing, Cam." He looked a little too pleased with himself and I didn't understand why, but I had no time to waste worrying about it. At that moment, I simply wanted to get home and back as quickly as possible.

I called a cab and accompanied Kyra back to our building, apologizing once again for leaving her alone with my colleagues for so long. She told me she thought I had just up and left without her, which is why she had come looking for me, and that made me feel even worse. Even though I had told her I'd asked her out that night simply as friends, abandoning her had still been a crappy thing to do. I did feel bad about it, but not enough to wish it hadn't happened. That little restroom hookup with Tonia would be worth feeling slightly awkward whenever I saw Kyra in the gym from then on.

After delivering her to her door like a gentleman, I headed back down to the lobby where I'd asked the taxi to wait for me. My hand had just grabbed the door handle to get back in the car when my phone rang.

Groaning, I pulled out my phone to check the number. The number belonged to a cell phone, one I didn't recognize, but my gut told me to answer it anyway.

"Hello?" As I answered, I sat back down in the back of the car and motioned for the driver to take me back to the bar.

"Cam, is that you?"

The voice sounded familiar but it took me a moment to place it. "Mrs Callahan?"

Why the heck would Tonia's mother be calling me? For a brief moment, I was suddenly transported back to those days in her basement when her parents would almost catch us, and absurdly, my heart rate spiked, imagining that she had called me because she knew what Tonia and I had done at the bar tonight.

Reminding myself that I was now a 24-year-old man who could do whatever I wanted, I tried to focus back on what she was saying.

"I'm so sorry to bother you, but we don't know that many people in Houston and since we just stayed with you last weekend and you were kind enough to give us your number, I thought it might be okay that I called."

Her words were rushed and hiccupped, and it felt like I had missed something, or she'd just left something out. She wasn't making any sense. "Of course it's okay. What's going on?"

"We... we're at the hospital."

My stomach immediately dropped and I held up my hand to get the driver's attention. "Which hospital?"

She gave me the name and I told the driver to head there instead even though I still didn't know what was happening.

"Is it Shawna?" I tried to guess. She should have gone home the day before, but things could have changed.

"No, no, Shawna's fine, but that's why I'm calling you instead of Dex. He's got enough to deal with."

Those words made me even more confused. She had said she didn't know many people in Houston, but I had assumed that meant besides her own children who lived here. Why would she be calling me rather than her own family?

"What's going on, Mrs Callahan?"

"It's Bill." She gave me the name of her husband, Tonia's father. "He had a heart attack this afternoon."

"Oh, gosh, ma'am." My shock made me revert to a 12-year-old boy, apparently, as the words shot out of my mouth. "Is he alright?"

"He's just resting now, they're still doing some tests, but we don't want to get anyone upset until we know more. Like I said, Dex's got enough going on right now."

I could understand that, but there seemed to be one other obvious person she could have called. "And Tonia?"

I could hear noise in the background as Mrs Callahan went silent, speaking to someone else for a moment before returning to the phone. "I've got to go, but if you're too busy..."

"I'm already on my way," I told her truthfully. "I'll be there as soon as I can."

~Tonia~

After cleaning myself up in the restroom, I returned to the bar where the Barnly Oil group were still drinking, laughing and talking, but I couldn't see either Cam or Kyra. Still glancing around for them as I sat down next to Tyler, I almost jumped as he put his hand on my shoulder.

"Cam asked me to tell you he had to leave but he'll be back later. Said he had something he wanted to talk to you about."

I couldn't hide the satisfaction that information gave me. It seemed I'd made an impression on him, at the very least, and maybe, at last, we could finally hash all of it out together. I still had no idea what the outcome would be, but at least we could both stop wondering. What happened the other night in his apartment and just a few minutes earlier in the restroom made it pretty clear to me that things weren't as resolved between us as we'd both believed, not to mention that I still wanted to talk to him about the things Marley had told me.

Maybe that night would be the night we could finally let it go.

The smile on my face made Tyler laugh. "I take it that something good happened during your extended absence?"

"None of your business," I told him, giving him a nudge as I tried not to look too pleased. Though I couldn't say for sure if Tyler's attentions played a role in what just happened, they didn't seem to have hurt. "Thank you for coming tonight, though. I owe you one."

"How about you let that woman at the end of the table know that you and I aren't really together, and we'll call it even?"

As I looked over to see who he meant, the woman quickly looked away, making it obvious she'd been watching us. Since it seemed pretty clear she was interested in Tyler, and apparently, he was interested too, that should be easy enough to deal with.

Giving Tyler a wink, I made my way over to chat with her, letting it drop casually that Tyler was just a friend, and then I went to sit with Marianne, giving the woman a chance to take my seat next to Tyler, which she quickly did.

It felt like high school all over again, and that impression didn't change once Marianne and I had a chance to catch up.

"Jason hasn't come over here at all yet," she told me unhappily. "He's just sitting over there with the other managers. Maybe I read too much into things."

I didn't think she had, and I also had a pretty good idea how we could find out for sure. "Come with me."

I pulled her to her feet and we both headed over to the bar to order some more drinks. As I expected, as soon as Marianne was separated from the rest of the women, Jason made his way over to us, coming up next to her at the bar before we'd even had a chance to put our order in.

"Are you ladies having a good time?" Though he smiled at me, he clearly meant the question for Marianne.

"It's been great," I told him, though I had no intention of sharing exactly why I had enjoyed myself so much. "Oh, shoot, I think I left my phone at the table. I'll be back in a minute. Go ahead and order without me."

Leaving them alone, I headed back to the table and took Marianne's old seat next to the other women while Jason and Marianne continued to chat by the bar and Tyler and the other woman were deep in conversation at the other end of the table.

That had to be some kind of matchmaking record. I was on fire that night. If only my own relationship was half as simple to sort out.

While I chatted with the other women from the office, half an hour passed since Cam left, and then another half hour. Marianne and Jason made their excuses and left, separately, but only a few minutes after each other, giving me a strong feeling that their evening wasn't over just yet.After another twenty minutes, Tyler asked if I minded if he left too. I told him to go ahead and thanked him again for coming in the first place. With a frown, I double-checked my phone just to be sure I hadn't missed any messages, but an empty screen stared back at me.

I couldn't imagine what would be keeping Cam so long. His apartment wasn't that far away; I knew that now that I knew exactly where he lived.

The crowd dwindled even further, and finally I had to face facts: Cam wasn't coming back and he hadn't even bothered to let me know. By the time I stood up to leave, my earlier satisfaction had completely dissipated.

Why did it feel like we were always on different wavelengths? When I needed some space, he took it personally, but when I wanted to get closer, he pulled away. I had tried to take Shawna's advice and not leave things unsaid, but how was I supposed to say them when he wouldn't listen?

Yes, he could make me come like a steam train rolling down a mountain, but what good was that if we still couldn't trust or open up to each other?

At some point, I really had to cut my losses and move on. I thought I *had* done that already before these last two weeks had ripped all the wounds open again, pressing on bruises that were still there, just beneath the surface, and as I walked out of the bar in frustration, I just wanted the numbness back that I had before. Where Cam had gone, who he'd gone with and what he might be doing there really didn't matter. What mattered was that he said he would come back and he didn't. Once more, he let me down.

At some point, it had to end, and I decided that evening would be it. I drew my line in the sand, and if he didn't like it, that was too fucking bad. Usually, I didn't give anyone a second chance, let alone a third one, and that evening showed exactly why. People didn't change, and to expect them to was a sign of madness.

When I got home, I turned my phone completely off and left it on the counter so I wouldn't be tempted to check later, and then I went to bed, alone, doing my best to put Cameron Bailey out of my head once and for all.

~Cam~

Mrs Callahan gave me a warm hug as soon as I arrived at the hospital room where Tonia's dad was recovering. He gave me a shaky smile from his bed, which seemed to me to be a good sign.

"How're you doing?" I asked him once Mrs Callahan let me go.

"I've been better," he said bluntly, his spirit obviously still intact even if his voice sounded far weaker than usual. "Thanks for coming, though I told her not to call you."

"He doesn't mind," Mrs Callahan replied on my behalf. "And you're going to need to start accepting some help now if you don't want this to happen again, or worse!"

Clearly, I'd walked into an ongoing argument, so I did my best to stay out of it while trying to figure out exactly why they'd asked me there in the first place.

"I understand why you didn't call Dex," I said, though I thought he'd probably still want to know, tough or not. "But what about Tonia or Laura? They'd both be here in a heartbeat."

Billie was still in college and didn't have a car, so it would be trickier for her, but the older two Callahan girls would drop everything for their daddy, I knew that for certain.

"I don't need them fussing and worrying," Mr Callahan replied sullenly. "One mother hen is bad enough, I don't need a whole brood."

Mrs Callahan pursed her lips at her husband, but she didn't respond directly to him, turning to me instead. "Right now, we really just need some help getting things in order."

Once again, I couldn't help thinking Tonia would be the obvious choice. "You think I can do better than Ms 'A Matter of Time' herself?"

That drew a smile from both of them, thankfully. "Tonia's the best, of course," her mom acknowledged. "But we need a practical head right now, not an emotional one."

As someone who had been on the receiving end of Tonia's emotional outbursts several times, I couldn't really argue about that. "What do you need me to do?"

Their request consisted of, as she'd said, mostly practical arrangements. The Callahans had been visiting friends not far from Houston when the heart attack happened, which explained why they ended up at the hospital there rather than in Sandy Creek. The ranch had been left in the hands of some of their hired help for the day, but Mr Callahan wouldn't be up to taking over again for some time, so plans needed to be put in place to ensure that things kept running smoothly until more permanent arrangements could be made.

Having me there to make the calls and deal with the business side of things left Mrs Callahan free to keep an eye on her husband and talk with the doctors when they came in to update them. Though I tried not to eavesdrop, I couldn't help overhearing a few things in the small hospital room, especially the part about the doctor suggesting retirement should be strongly considered.

Mr Callahan had worked himself into a huff by the time the doctor left. "I'm only 52," he pointed out angrily to no one in particular. "I ain't retiring yet."

"Bobby Jenkins died last year at 48," his wife shot back. "You think that's better than retiring a few years early?"

As they argued, I glanced up at the clock on the wall, and my stomach sank as I saw it had been almost an hour already since I left the bar. I needed to get Tonia a message so she didn't think I stood her up. Since the Callahans were distracted, I pulled out my phone and started typing.

Hey, I'm just taking care of something but I'm still coming back. If you'd rather head home, I can come to your place instead, just send me the address. I still want to...

Mid-sentence, the screen went black.

Shit.

I had seen the low-battery warning when I was on the last call but I thought I had more time left than that.

"Mr and Mrs Callahan?" I hated to interrupt the argument still in progress, but this was important. "My phone just died and I need to send Tonia a message. I told her I'd be in touch with her tonight. Can I borrow one of yours?"

The two of them exchanged glances. "If you send her a message on my phone, she'll know you're with me," Mrs Callahan pointed out. "And for right now, until we figure this all out, we'd rather none of the kids know anything about it."

My stomach sank even further. "You don't expect me to keep this from Tonia?"

"Only for a day," Mr Callahan piped up. "We're going to Dex's gallery tomorrow, we'll figure out what we want to say to them all by then."

"That's only if the doctor clears you to go," his wife pointed out.

They continued to argue with their eyes before Mrs Callahan sighed and turned back to me.

"I think I've got a charging cord in my purse." That was the first bit of bright news I'd got since arriving here, but my excitement quickly faded as we realized it didn't fit my phone. "Oh shoot, I'm sorry, Cam, but don't worry about Tonia. She'll understand."

I didn't feel anywhere near as confident of that fact as they seemed to. However, maybe if I left right then, I could still get back to the bar before everyone left.

"Is there anything else you need for tonight, then?"

They told me everything was under control and asked me again to keep everything to myself until the following evening. I gave vague assurances but made no actual promises before I headed back down to the taxi rank outside. Traffic had never seemed as slow as it did on the way back downtown, and as soon as we reached the bar, I threw my cash at the driver, telling him to keep the change as I hopped out and ran back inside.

Frustration soon washed over me yet again as I realized she was gone. The entire group had left and the space where we'd been sitting had been occupied by a different group.

Cursing my luck and my timing and anything else I could think of, I made my way home and finally plugged my phone in. As soon as I could turn it on, I retyped my message, telling her I was at home but still wanted to talk and would come to her.

No reply came through. The message stayed unread, and when I tried calling her a few minutes later, it went straight to voicemail. Tonia's cheery message made me feel even worse and I hung up without leaving one of my own.

The time was getting late and if it were any other day and any other woman, I would say that I'd wait and talk about it with her in the morning, but I'd made that mistake with Tonia before. The more time she had alone, the more she would get in her head and second-guess what happened between us that night and whether she wanted to talk to me about it at all.

I wouldn't let that happen again. If she decided to reject me again, it wouldn't be because of a lack of information. It was long past time we got all of this out into the open.

"Cam?" Dex's sleep-filled voice made my guilt rise again as he picked up on the fourth ring. He and Shawna were probably exhausted and already in bed. "What's going on?"

"I'm really sorry to call you so late, but Tonia's got her phone off and I need to talk to her. Can you get me her address?"

"What year is this?" he grumbled, but I could hear the bed creak as he got up. He must know I wouldn't be calling if it weren't important. "Hold on a sec."

I did my best to hold on, though I felt just about ready to jump out of my skin, anticipation and nerves battling inside me. Whatever happened when I went to her apartment would settle this madness between us once and for all, I felt pretty damn certain of that, but which way it might go, I truly couldn't guess.

"Here you go." Dex read out an address to me and I repeated it back twice, making extra sure that I hadn't missed anything.

"Thanks, Dex. I really appreciate it."

"No problem." There was a slight pause before he added a few more words, said with almost brotherly compassion. "Good luck, Cam."

Chapter Eleven

~**Tonia**~

As I rolled over in bed for the hundredth time, trying to get comfortable in my bed that normally felt perfect for me but that night didn't seem to suit me at all, the buzzer rang for my apartment. When someone buzzed up to my apartment from the building's front door, the notification would go to my phone first, but if the person waiting hit it again within the same minute, then it rang out on the building's intercom system.

That meant someone had to have hit the button for my apartment at least twice, but it must have been a mistake. I wasn't expecting anyone, and as I rolled over yet again, I could see the clock on my bedside table telling me it was almost midnight.

Convinced that the notification wasn't really for me, I tried once again to close my eyes, but before long, the buzzer sounded again. Whoever was down there meant business, and my stomach suddenly sank as I wondered if something had happened to Shawna? Maybe my family had been trying to reach me and couldn't because I had left my phone off.

That was stupid and selfish of me, I admonished myself as I jumped out of bed and ran to the intercom by the front door. "Hello?"

"Tonia, it's Cam."

His was pretty much the last voice I expected to hear, and for a moment, I wondered if I might be dreaming. Maybe I had actually fallen asleep after all. "How do you know where I live?"

"It's a long story, but I'm here now and we need to talk."

He was right, and I *knew* he was right, but the way he disappeared earlier still stung. "You were supposed to come back and talk to me at the bar tonight."

"I know that." The frustration in his voice came through loud and clear even through the tinny speaker. "And I know you're hurt and defensive because I didn't. I know you, Sugar, but I can explain everything if you just give me a chance."

Those words sent me hurtling back into the past, to the last time he said something like that to me, almost word for word.

Standing in the school hallway, my whole body froze as Kara Beckett walked up and announced to me and everyone else within earshot that Cam would be taking Marley Stevens to the prom.

"I just got it straight from the horse's mouth," she said, barely able to contain her glee at being the one who got to break the news to me. "Looks like you'll need to find yourself a new date, though anyone worth going with is already taken."

The words went into my ears, but they didn't fully register. An odd ringing sensation had taken over my head as my heart pounded and my limbs went weak. Could I be having a heart attack, I wondered? Or maybe the explanation was less dramatic but just as painful; maybe my heart was simply breaking.

Although I had gone to school that morning full of fire and ready to give Cam a piece of my mind for lying to me and what I'd seen at Marley's house the night before, a part of me still hoped he had a good explanation for all of it. Deep down, I hoped that he would tell me I had it wrong, that I'd make a mistake, and the rest of what he'd always said to me about us being meant to be together and standing the test of time, those were the things that were true.

Now, those hopes lay shattered at my feet, crushed beneath Kara Beckett's high-heeled boots as she and her friends smirked and whispered, bearing witness to my heartbreak like it had been designed for their entertainment.

The fire that had been raging in me was engulfed in ice-cold humiliation, and when the two met, they solidified like lava hitting the sea, turning into something hard and permanent, encasing my broken heart in stone.

The whispers grew louder around me and the crowd parted as Cam appeared at the end of the hall and made his way over to me.

Every eye was on him, but if he noticed, he didn't seem to care. His attention was fixed entirely on me, his deep brown eyes conflicted and troubled.

"Tonia, I need to talk to you."

His voice was quiet, making it clear he did, in fact, know that everyone else was listening. Perhaps going somewhere in private with him to talk would have been the smarter option, but I didn't want to give him the easy way out. He lied to me and he cheated on me, and if he thought I would let him get away with it and break up with me without a scene, then he didn't know me very well at all.

Everyone already knew what he'd done and how I'd been pushed aside. My mortification had already gone about as deep as it could go; I'd been cut down so low, all I could think about was taking him down with me.

"Is it true? Did you ask Marley to the prom?"

My voice was *not* quiet; it rang out loud and strong, making sure not a single person in the unnatural silence of the hallway missed a word I said.

Gasps and whispers circled around us, and Cam glanced furtively from side to side, his jaw set, before taking a step closer to me. "Please, let's go and talk..."

"It's a yes or no answer," I snapped at him, folding my arms tightly across my chest. "Which is it?"

His lips pressed tightly together as something like regret danced in his eyes, but we'd gone way past that point. I just wanted the truth. "Yes, but it's not what you think. Let me explain what's going on."

All I really heard was the 'yes'. My friends told me the rest later. I wasn't even really aware of going up and slapping him across the face until my hand started stinging from the force of it.

"You lied to me. You bastard! You said you'd never hurt me. You said you'd *never* cheat on me. Was every fucking word you ever said to me a lie?"

He blinked as tears gathered in the corners of his eyes. I couldn't say if they were because of what I said, what he'd done, or the slap I'd just given him. It must have hurt since I didn't hold back. I wanted it to hurt.

"Ms Callahan, Mr Bailey, my office, now!" The principal's angry voice boomed out down the hall as everyone else quickly dispersed, still whispering amongst themselves. No one would be forgetting the show they'd just witnessed any time soon.

My heart still racing and my blood boiling as it ran through my veins, I followed the principal to his office where he told me and Cam to take a seat.

"Do you want to tell me what that was about? Violence is not tolerated in the school and neither is swearing. As class president, you know that, Tonia."

Of course I did, but at that moment, I had never cared about anything less. All I felt was anger; well, anger *and* pain, and I wanted Cam to feel it too. I wanted him to hurt just as bad as he hurt me.

"You want to know what it was about? It was about my *ex*-boyfriend cheating on me and asking another girl to prom without having the decency to even break up with me first."

Genuine dismay crossed the principal's face. At such a small school, he knew all the students pretty well. He definitely knew all about our relationship and up until now, we had been a model couple.

"Cam, is that true?" he asked cautiously.

"He admitted it to me!" I interjected before Cam could get a word out. "I just asked him out in the hall and he said yes. That's why I hit him, and I won't apologize for it because I'm not sorry."

"I've already heard you, Tonia," the principal told me before turning back to Cam. "Is there anything you want to add?"

"I never cheated on her." His words were quiet, his voice raw and almost broken. "I wouldn't do that. If we're broken up, it's only because she's the one doing the breaking."

"So why does she think you cheated?" The principal was trying to keep us both calm, but it wasn't really working.

Cam's reply was sullen, drifting into bitterness. "Apparently, she doesn't trust me. She would rather take Kara Beckett's word over mine."

My anger boiled over once again as I screamed directly at him. "You fucking admitted it!"

"Language, Tonia." The principal's look of disapproval grew stronger. "That's your last warning. We can discuss this civilly, or I can call your parents."

How did he expect me to behave 'civilly' after what Cam did? There was nothing civil about any of this but I tried my best to hold my tongue, sitting back in my chair, still seething.

The principal tried one more time to steer us towards some kind of resolution. "Do you have any reason to think that Cam's lying beside what Kara Beckett said?"

I had plenty. "There's the fact that he told me straight out that he barely knew Marley Stevens, and yet he was at her house last night. I saw him myself."

Cam's expression turned harder as he looked over at me. "Were you following me?"

Indignation flared up yet again. "You're damn right I was, and it turned out I had good reason to! I saw you in her room."

He looked at me almost like he'd never seen me before. "That's really what you think?"

"What else am I supposed to think? You haven't given me any other explanation."

The same fire inside me burned in his eyes as well. I recognized that stubborn, pigheaded look of his; I'd seen it in action plenty of times, he'd just never used it on me before. "I wanted to. That's what I wanted to talk to you about this morning instead of blowing it up in front of the whole school."

"Well, let's hear it then. Let's hear your explanation." I crossed my arms again, and he did the same, mocking me even further as he repeated the gesture.

"No. I'm not going to tell you until you apologize for all of this. You know me better than that, Tonia. You know I wouldn't do that. I can't believe, after everything we've been through, that you wouldn't give me a chance to explain before jumping to the worst possible conclusion."

"You want *me* to fucking apologize?"

That was the last straw for the principal. "Alright, Tonia, you're going to take a few days at home to cool off. Cameron, you can get to class. We won't involve the police unless you want to press charges."

"*He* can press charges?" I squealed in fury.

"You're the one who hit him," the principal reminded me before turning back to Cam. "Well?"

Cam just shook his head. "No charges. All I want is an apology."

His eyes pierced into me for a second more, filled with hurt and sadness, before he got up and walked out the door.

"You still there, Tonia? You going to let me up?" Cam's voice brought me back to the present as it echoed once more through my intercom, and I shook my head to shake away the memories of the past.

After speaking to Marley earlier that week, I knew now that there *had* been more to the story than I'd known at the time. Maybe the reason had been good enough and maybe it hadn't, but there had been an explanation. Using the same logic, maybe Cam did have an explanation for where he'd been that night after leaving the bar. It didn't mean I had to accept it, but at least I could hear him out and make up my mind with all the facts.

We had, after all, grown up a lot since high school, even if at times over the past couple of weeks, it didn't entirely feel like it.

"You've got five minutes," I told him, hitting the button to open the door for him. "Hurry up."

~Cam~

I anticipated more of a fight. I half expected her to make me stand there in the lobby and tell her what I came to say over the intercom, or to refuse to speak to me at all. I was prepared to stand there until someone else came in or out of the building, beg them to let me in, and make my way to her door where she couldn't ignore me quite so easily.

So, when the door buzzed and she told me to come up, I was genuinely surprised but grateful too. Maybe she wasn't the only one who had figured out that we needed to change our approach if we were ever going to get out of this pattern we were stuck in.

Flinging the unlocked door open, I headed to the elevator. Her building didn't require a key to get to the floor so I was able to go on up on my own. Tonia's apartment was on the 14th floor and my heart pounded in rhythm with the shrill dings that marked each floor along the way.

The door already sat open when I reached her apartment, just enough that I could push my way in without knocking. She didn't plan on wasting any time, apparently. She said she would only give me five minutes, but I wasn't too worried about that. Once I got in front of her, once we got talking, I had a feeling she would want to see it through to the end, just as I did.

"Tonia?" I called out her name as soon as I got inside and closed the door behind me. In front of me, a door led to a bathroom, and a hallway stretched out to the left. Even at the front door, I could see that everything was neat and organized, just as I would have expected. The toiletries in the bathroom were lined up and her shoes, other than the one that had been holding the door open, were all neatly arranged on a rack with dress shoes on one side and casual shoes on the other, everything in its place, as efficient as can be.

"In the kitchen," came her reply from down the hall, so I kicked off my own shoes and followed the sound of her voice.

The lights were low further inside, allowing the city lights to creep in through the living room windows. I found Tonia sitting on a stool at the counter that bridged the kitchen and the living room, her bare legs crossed beneath the peach-coloured silky nightgown she wore that only went to her mid-thighs, the lacy trim at the top drawing attention to the perfect swell of her breasts, and all the blood in my body immediately diverted to my groin. Was she *trying* to drive me crazy? Just like that, my mind filled with images and memories of what happened in the restroom earlier, and what happened at my apartment earlier that week.

It would be so easy to give in to the nearly overwhelming desire for her that flared up inside me, but that wouldn't get us anywhere, as we'd already learned. We needed to talk, and so I went to sit on the other side of the counter from her, far from temptation.

Tonia gave me a small smirk as I took my seat, as if she knew exactly why I'd chosen to sit there. "Tea?" she offered. "It's non-caffeinated."

She did indeed have a cup of tea in front of her, which I hadn't noticed before. I'd been a little distracted by everything else about her. I'd barely registered anything about the sleek kitchen behind her, everything perfectly in its place, or the living room behind me. A large painting took up most of one wall, probably painted by Dex, but beyond that, all I could see in the whole apartment was her.

In any case, I hadn't come there for tea. "No, thanks. Listen, I'm sorry for not coming back to the bar tonight. I tried to text you but my phone died, and by the time I got back there, you'd already left. I sent you a text as soon as I got home, but your phone must have been off."

She reached over and tapped the screen on the device which sat next to her on the counter. "Yeah, I just turned it back on. I saw your message. Are you going to tell me how you got my address?"

"From Dex," I told her honestly. No point in hiding that when he'd probably tell her himself.

"And where did you go when you left the bar? Did you and Kyra lose track of time?"

Unmistakable jealousy ran through her voice, and it heartened me to hear it. She had no reason or right to be jealous, but she was anyway, and I knew just how that felt. I'd felt it all night when I watched her and Tyler.

"Do you really believe that, Sugar? You think after what happened in that restroom that I went home and jumped into bed with another woman?"

I could practically see the smart retort on the tip of her tongue, the defensiveness and the need to not show even a hint of vulnerability, but to my surprise, she held it in. She took a sip of her tea, swallowing her comeback along with it, and shook her head instead. "No, I don't think you were with Kyra. So, where were you?"

This was the moment of truth, quite literally. All those years ago, when she asked if I knew Marley, I lied. I put the promise I made to Marley ahead of the promise I made to Tonia to always be honest with her. And though I still thought she'd been in the wrong for jumping to conclusions later on and not giving me a chance to explain, I had to accept the blame for my part in the whole mess. If I had just answered that damn question honestly, maybe none of the rest of it would have ever happened.

It was not a mistake I intended to repeat, and so I told her the truth. "I was at the hospital with your parents."

Her eyes widened in surprise or disbelief, I couldn't tell which. Maybe both. "What are you talking about?"

"First of all, everyone's doing okay, so don't panic. Your dad had a heart attack earlier today."

Despite me just saying not to panic, Tonia looked right on the edge of it. She snatched her phone back off the counter, and though I didn't know for sure who she intended to call, I grabbed it out of her hands before she could call anyone.

"Give that back, Cam. Right now." Her eyes flashed with fire as she tried to reach over and take it back from me, her teacup clattering dangerously on its saucer as she brushed up against it.

"Not until you hear me out, Sugar. They told me not to tell you, but I'm telling you anyway because I don't want there to be any more secrets between us, alright?"

A dozen different emotions swam in those pretty blue eyes as she processed everything I'd just told her, but finally, she leaned back, letting her hands fall to the counter again. "What happened? Why would they call you?"

Trying not to leave anything out, I told her everything they shared with me about what happened and what I'd helped them with while I was there. "They said they were going to tell y'all tomorrow. I guess you're getting together at Dex's new gallery?"

She nodded in confirmation before shaking her head as she thought things over. "This is going to kill Dex, on top of everything else he's going through."

Her choice of words made us both wince. Death certainly seemed to be hovering around the Callahan clan, even if it hadn't made its move just yet.

It did help me try to explain her parent's motivation to her, at least. "I'm pretty sure that's why your parents didn't call him tonight, or any of you. They didn't want you to worry until they knew more about exactly what was going on. By tomorrow, they should know what all the tests showed and what your dad's gotta do to get better."

We both fell silent for a moment as she considered everything I'd just revealed, and since she seemed to have calmed down, I placed her phone back on the counter and slid it over to the middle where she could reach it if she wanted to.

It remained untouched.

"Why didn't you tell me the truth about Marley?"

The question seemed to come out of nowhere, and yet, it made perfect sense to me too. I'd just trusted her with something meant to be a secret, so she wanted to know why I hadn't done the same all those years ago.

Just as I had when I answered her earlier question, I held nothing back. "I promised her I wouldn't. She asked me to keep the secret and I thought I was doing the right thing. When you asked me if I knew her, I didn't know you were having doubts about us, so I lied to try to protect her, and that was a mistake. I planned to tell you that morning when I got to the school. When I asked to talk to you, that was exactly what I wanted to talk about. I would have told you everything then, I just never got the chance to."

Tonia nodded, her eyes focused on the cup of tea in her hands rather than on me, but I knew she was listening carefully to every word. "What would you have said?"

The words were almost ingrained in my head even though I'd never spoken them out loud. I'd rehearsed them over and over that morning as I showered and got ready and while I walked to the school. I'd tried a dozen different ways to approach it before I decided on the one I figured would be best.

"I was going to say: I'm sorry, Sugar. I've made a mess of things and I need your help. I've been trying to do a good thing, but I'm over my head now and I know you'll know what to do. You always do."

Her eyes flitted up to me, just for a moment, before returning to her cup. In the dim light of the room, the expression in them almost looked like regret.

I carried on as if I were talking to her six years ago rather than the Tonia sitting in her Houston apartment. "You know you asked the other day if I know Marley Stevens? Fact is, I've been getting to know her.

Her mama's sick and her daddy's up in the city, and she's not in a good place. I've been trying to help her out but I'm losing control. She wants me to take her to the prom so she's got some good memories to share with her mama, but I can't do that. You know there's no one I want to go with but you."

"Then why did you tell her you would?" Tonia's voice was quiet, speaking down to the counter instead of to me, but I heard her perfectly fine anyway.

"I tried to tell her no and she started talking about wanting to die like her mama. I was scared, Sugar. I thought she might do something crazy. So, I said yes, but that's why I need your help now. I need to find a way out of this so Marley doesn't get hurt but you and I still get to have the prom we always imagined. I know: I'm an idiot, and I've made a right mess of all of it, but you can help me fix it. I know you can. I'm sorry I didn't come to you right from the start."

Those blue eyes looked up at me again, but that time, they stayed locked on me as she weighed the truth in my words. "You weren't going to take her? Honestly? She thought you were."

"She thought that because I lied to her. I was never going to take her, Tonia. I never for a second wanted to go with anyone other than you."

Her lips twitched and she pressed them tighter together, trying to control whatever she might be feeling at that moment. I honestly couldn't even begin to guess what that might be.

When she stayed silent for a while, I spoke up again. "Can I ask you a question too, Sugar?"

She nodded, still not saying anything.

"Why did you think I cheated on you? How could you think that?" I tried to keep my tone as neutral as possible, with a great deal of effort. That was the one thing I had never fully been able to understand.

"You started avoiding me. You were never at home, never wanted to come over, and then you lied to my face. You told me you didn't even know her, and then I saw you at her house. I saw you holding her in her room, and the next day she told the whole school you were taking her to prom."

That all looked bad, I had to admit, but she had missed the heart of my question. "That's not what I mean, Tonia. Those are the reasons someone else might have thought I was cheating. Why did *you* think it? Didn't you know no other woman in the world came close to you for me? Didn't you know just how goddamn much I love you?"

There were tears in my eyes as the hurt of the past bubbled up to the surface again, but there was no anger in my pain anymore. All that remained was sadness: sadness for the heartbroken kid I'd been and sadness for all the time we'd lost. If we'd just had this conversation six years earlier, how different might things have turned out?

Only as my words faded into the stillness of the room and as Tonia's blue eyes looked over at me in uncertainty did I realize exactly what I said.

I used the present tense. I didn't say I *loved* her. I said I *love* her.

And I had no idea what she would say back.

~Tonia~

The look on Cam's face broke my heart, but not as much as the words he just said. I didn't miss that he used the word 'love' in the present tense, but I didn't intend to read too much into it, not when there was so much I needed to unpack in the rest of his words.

All those years, I never understood why he was so damn insistent on an apology. I thought he was upset for the way I had called him out in front of the whole school, breaking up in the most public way possible. I thought he resented the fact that I wouldn't give him a second chance.

And I most certainly thought that *he* owed *me* an apology, not the other way around.

Even after what Marley revealed to me earlier that week, I didn't fully understand. It made sense to me that he'd be upset that I thought he cheated when he didn't, but I couldn't understand why the apology was such a sticking point. If he loved me, he should have fought for me whether I apologized or not.

But with the words he'd just spoken, finally, after all this time, I could see where he was coming from.

He thought that I didn't love him as much as he loved me. He took my refusal to apologize as a sign that I gave up on us first, even though in my mind it had always been him that set everything in motion.

We'd both been so caught up in our own hurt that we forgot to consider what the other person felt, which was what love was supposed to be about in the first place.

I did my best to explain myself to him, six years too late. "It was because you loved me so much that I believed it."

He squeezed his eyes closed, his hands going to his temples as he processed my words. "You're going to have to break that down for me, Sugar. I don't understand what that means."

Those were the feelings I had tried to pin down the other night when I ran out on him after we slept together. Knowing just how good we still were together and remembering just how good it had always been, and then hearing him ask for an apology again, I needed time to think it all through. And the main question I asked myself was exactly the one he had just asked me: why did I believe he had cheated on me?

I had some evidence, of course, but I could have questioned it more. So why didn't I? Why was I so sure I knew exactly what had happened?

Some of it came down to my Callahan genes, that couldn't be denied, but that didn't fully explain it either. I'd wanted to talk to him about it the next morning in his office, when he turned me away, and I tried to find the words again in the soft light of my kitchen as the clock took us into the new day.

"You were my whole world, Cam. I never even thought about anyone else. When you kissed me that day out on that dirt road, that was it for me. You were my first everything and when you told me you loved me, I didn't think I would ever need anything else."

He fidgeted in his seat, obviously torn between staying where he was and not interrupting me, and getting up so he could come around to my side of the counter, closing the space between us. For the moment, at least, he stayed put.

"My whole future, my whole life was wrapped up in you, and that felt exhilarating but scary too. Somewhere deep inside, I was afraid that I loved you more than you loved me, and that as soon as we were out of that little town, you were going to realize that the world was a whole lot bigger than me."

His brow furrowed as I spoke and he couldn't help interjecting: "You never said anything like that to me."

"Because I knew what you'd say. You'd tell me how sure you were, how nothing would ever happen to come between us. You never wanted to talk about the 'what if's. You were so damn certain all the time."

"And that's a bad thing?" He still looked confused. "I was sure because I loved you."

"I know that, but I also knew how hard you found it to admit you were wrong about anything. So, when you started sneaking around and avoiding me, I thought: this is exactly what Cam would do if he were cheating on me. He would deny it as long as he could, because otherwise he'd have to admit he'd been wrong. And when you lied to me about Marley, that seemed like further proof. You said you wouldn't lie to me, but you did, and if you could break that promise, how could I trust any of them? It all unravelled from there until eventually I couldn't see any other possibility. And that morning in the school, I lashed out at you because the idea that your love was a lie broke my heart, Cam. It broke it so badly that I didn't even care if you were hurting too. I just didn't want to hurt alone."

His fists were clenched, his face half-hidden in the shadows of the living room, but even so, I could see the tears in his eyes, the same as the ones shimmering in my own line of vision.

"I'm sorry, Tonia." The words were rough and raw, coming from somewhere deep inside him. "I didn't think of it that way."

I nodded, trying to keep my own voice steady. "I know you didn't. You were just trying to help someone out, which is who you are, through and through. I'm sorry I didn't let you explain."

Those simple words had taken six long years to get to, but at last, they'd been said. We had both made mistakes, and we both took responsibility for them.

And as soon as they were out of my mouth, Cam got to his feet, circling the counter to come over to me. His hands were on my face as he moved towards me, leaving me in no doubt of what he wanted, but at the last second, I turned away.

"I think you should go."

I could sense his muscles tightening even though I wasn't looking at him. "Why?" he asked hoarsely.

"Because we keep doing this. We keep running before we've walked. You could come to my bed now, but I don't know what it would mean. I think we both need to take a step back, think about everything that was said tonight, and decide what we want. Because I can't do this part-way with you, Cam. You aren't casual to me, and you never have been."

His hands dropped as he took a step back, and as I turned to face him, I could see the conflict playing out on his face. He knew I was right, even if our bodies were both screaming otherwise. The evidence of his arousal was clear, and my heart pounded, fuelling the steady pulse between my legs.

But before I fell into his arms again, before I let myself believe our story might not be over yet, I needed to know what he wanted. We'd talked through the past, but we still needed to sort out the present, and maybe even the future too, and I didn't want to rush it.

At length, Cam nodded. "I understand, Sugar. You aren't casual to me either. If we're going to do this again, we're going to do it right."

That was exactly what I was hoping for, even if I wasn't ready to admit it to anyone just yet, not even myself.

"I'll see you in the office tomorrow." He took my hand, pressing it to his lips like an old-fashioned gentleman before he turned and headed back down the hall, letting himself out.

My tea went cold as I continued to sit there in the lingering scent of his cologne and the dim midnight light. As much as I wanted him to be sure, I needed to be sure too. Could I really give Cam my heart again?

Or, as seemed far more likely, was there a part of it that had never left his keeping?

Chapter Twelve

~**Cam**~

Sleep refused to come when I got home, even though I knew I had to get up in the morning for work. After everything that just happened, my mind wouldn't turn off, so I went down to the gym in my building instead, running on the treadmill to burn off my excess energy as I tried to sort through what I felt and what I thought about everything that had been said between us that night.

She apologized. After six very long years, Tonia Callahan actually looked me in the eye and said she was sorry.

So many things she said were a surprise to me. I never knew that she'd had any doubts about us going the distance; honestly, I didn't. All through high school, I just assumed we were going to get married and be together forever. I thought she felt that too, but instead of certainty on my part, she saw single-mindedness and rigidity, and she was afraid it would one day work against her.

And it did, though not in the way she thought. It worked against us both when I refused to see things from her point of view and try to understand why she reacted the way she did. I only saw her lack of trust in me; I didn't see the crack that I'd caused first by that stupid lie I told.

So, when I sat there in her apartment and told her I was sorry, I truly meant it. Maybe that was why, after all that time, she said it too. Those two simple words were all I'd wanted, and with them, I finally felt like the scars of the past were truly starting to heal.

Not to mention that I could definitely tease her later about the fact that I said it first, if we did get back together. *If we did get back together...*

Was that really a possibility? Even after the incredible sex we had the other night, I didn't let myself go there in my mind. I couldn't set myself up for that kind of disappointment if we weren't on the same page.

However, when she sent me away earlier that night, when she stopped me from kissing her even though I felt sure she wanted me as much as I wanted her, she did it so that we *could* really think this through. So, what if I did let myself think about it, if I stopped to ask myself if I wanted to be with her again?

With sweat dripping down the back of my neck, my lungs burning and my muscles protesting the punishing pace I'd set myself, I didn't see how I could deny it.

Of course I wanted to be with Tonia. I always had, from that very first kiss out on the dirt road, and even before then.

From the very first time we met, something about her drew me in. With her, everything felt stronger, brighter, and a little more real. The past ten days, ever since she pushed that restroom door open onto my toe on Monday morning last week, my emotions had been all over the place. I'd felt a hundred different things, been exhausted and invigorated, angry and scared, but not for one second had I felt the least bit apathetic.

Nothing was ever boring with Tonia around.

Yes, she had her flaws, and yes, she'd made mistakes, but I'd made mistakes too and I sure as hell knew I wasn't perfect either.

Was it crazy to think we could pick up right where we left off? We certainly had in the bedroom. Although I'd been with other women while we were apart, when I was inside her, I honestly couldn't remember how it felt with anyone else.

There must have been changes in her life over the last six years, but everything I'd seen over the last week and a half told me that deep down, she was still the same person, just a little older and wiser. And if we worked back then, why the hell wouldn't we work now that we'd finally made amends?

By the time the machine came to a rest at the end of the cycle I'd programmed, I'd made up my mind: I wanted to give us a shot. Not casually, not part way; I wanted Tonia to be mine, and I would tell her so.

Until then, I just had to hope that she didn't have one of her trademark changes of mood before I could get the words out.

My alarm in the morning should have been unwelcome considering I had no more than four hours' sleep, but I sprang out of bed as if I'd had a full night's sleep. I left my apartment early, in plenty of time to stop off for a blueberry muffin for the woman I had a meeting with first thing that morning. We were supposed to be working on my organizational methods, but I hoped we could talk about us instead.

Making small talk with my colleagues felt like torture as my head turned to the door every time someone came in, hoping to see Tonia's blonde head at the door, but as it ticked closer to nine o'clock, there was still no sign of her.

Everyone drifted to their own desks and I went to my office as well, pulling out my phone to make sure I had no missed message. I'd made sure to fully charge my phone overnight, but nothing waited for me there. The reminder about my appointment popped up as I logged into my computer, and I frowned as I looked over at the door again.

Tonia was never late. Something must be wrong.

Locking my computer, I got to my feet and went to Jason's office where he and Marianne were sitting side-by-side, looking considerably cozier than they had before last night.

"Good morning," I called out from the door, not wanting to startle them, but they both leaned away from each other guiltily anyway. "Sorry to interrupt, but you haven't heard anything from Tonia Callahan, have you? I'm supposed to be meeting with her this morning and she's not here."

"Oh, I'm so sorry, I forgot," Marianne stammered as she got to her feet. "I was supposed to tell you. She called me this morning to say she couldn't make it in. She had a family emergency."

An emergency? Did something happen with her dad, or with Shawna? "Is everyone okay?"

"I don't know," she told me apologetically. "She just said that she wouldn't be in today and to let you know specifically. I'm so sorry, I got distracted."

She glanced back down at Jason, making it clear what had distracted her, but that wasn't my concern right now. I wanted to know what kept Tonia away from the office, and why she hadn't got in touch with me herself.

"It's alright. Thanks for letting me know."

Giving them both a nod, I returned to my office where I pulled out my phone and sent Tonia a text.

Everything okay, Sugar?

It went to read almost immediately, letting me know she definitely had her phone with her, and a moment later, her reply popped up.

It's okay. I'm at the hospital with my dad. There's no change, but he's mad at you for telling me.

Great. Getting on the bad side of yet another Callahan was just what I needed.

As if she'd heard my thoughts, she sent through one more line: *I'm glad you did, though.*

I was glad too, but her words and actions weren't quite lining up. *Why are you avoiding me, then?*

I'm not. I'm still thinking, as we discussed, and in the meantime, I followed proper protocols for alerting the business to my absence.

My eyes couldn't have rolled any harder. *I think we're past proper protocols, Tonia. And I'm ready to talk.*

Was she really not sure what she wanted? What was holding her back?

Let's give it the weekend, she suggested, and immediately I shook my head, though she couldn't see me. She had stuff going on with her family,

I got that, but I had no intention of giving her a chance to second guess herself and think of all the reasons we shouldn't do this. I wanted her to remember the one damn good reason we should.

Arguing with her about it over text wouldn't accomplish anything, though. She'd dig in harder, like she always did. I knew her, and that was an advantage I intended to use.

So, I simply wrote a few words back to her, pretending to give in, even though in reality, I was doing no such thing: *If you say so, Sugar.*

I had one other advantage too: I knew exactly where she planned to be that night. All I had to do was turn up.

~Tonia~

My mom watched me like a hawk as I put my phone away. "Was that Cam? What's going on with you two?"

If I knew how to answer that question, I wouldn't be at the hospital.

After he left the night before, I sat at the counter for a long time. I felt closer to Cam there since it was the only place in my apartment he'd ever been, and I wanted to hold onto that feeling as I thought over what I wanted.

But the longer I sat there, the more I realized that wasn't what I needed. When Cam and I were together, we were fine; that had never been the issue. Our troubles came when we were apart and we had time to overthink. I was guilty of that as much as him; it was part of the reason I'd convinced myself he cheated on me in the first place, and it explained why he refused to talk to me earlier that week after we slept together.

On our own, we got in our own heads and created our own problems, and that was exactly why I'd sent him away in the first place. I needed to know he wouldn't change his mind, and I needed to be sure I wouldn't either.

One night wasn't enough to be certain of that, so when the morning came and I was faced with the prospect of going into the office and seeing him there, I simply decided not to. We needed more time; we needed a proper test of what the distance would do to us after all of the turmoil and emotional and physical upheaval of the last few days.

The weekend should be just about enough time. By Monday, hopefully, I would have it all figured out.

Even better, I had a built-in excuse to get out of work as I did have a family member in the hospital, one who hadn't impressed me by going to my ex-boyfriend instead of me for help. So, instead of going to work, I left a message with Marianne and headed to the hospital instead. It didn't take me long to find my dad's room, and my mom and dad both looked up in surprise as I walked in.

"That boy didn't keep his mouth shut, did he?" my dad grumbled.

Cam was hardly a boy anymore, but I supposed to my dad, he always would be. His comment meant he was feeling good enough to be complaining, which meant I didn't have to hold back either.

"You shouldn't have asked him to! How would you feel if I ended up in the hospital and didn't tell you until after I got out?" I fixed him with a stern look, crossing my arms firmly.

"Honestly, I'd be glad that you saved me the worry, which is all we were tryin' to do for you." His glare was just as strong as mine, and neither of us looked ready to back down until my mom stepped in.

"Alright, let's check the Callahan tempers at the door. Tonia, your dad's still recovering, go easy on him. Jim, your daughter's just worried about you, though she has a funny way of showing it."

That was an interesting choice of words. Maybe I *did* have a funny way of showing I cared about someone.

The people I loved were the ones who made me angriest. I'd check my words around other people, usually, but when it came to my family or my closest friends, or Cam, I let them feel the full brunt of my passion, good or bad.

Cam never got mad at me for that. In fact, he usually rose to the challenge, arguing back with me or supporting me when we were on the same side. Maybe somewhere deep down, he knew that I wouldn't get so worked up if I didn't care.

Maybe, deep down, he'd always understood me.

"What did Cam tell you about your dad?" my mom asked, and I relayed everything he'd said, which she confirmed was pretty much the whole story. The nurses were feeling positive that my dad would be discharged that day, though there were going to be some lifestyle adjustments needed.

"Are you really going to retire?" I asked in shock when my mom mentioned the possibility. I couldn't imagine my dad not working on the ranch; it had always been his whole life.

"I'm... thinking about it," he admitted, though I could see just how much it pained him to even consider it. "Your mom and I talked it over last night and she made some good points. I want to be around for the good stuff in your lives, and if that means slowing down a bit, then I guess that's what I'm gonna have to do."

My mom squeezed his hand in appreciation and support. She also knew just how hard it would be for him, but she appreciated him considering it too. Sometimes, we had to make sacrifices for the people we cared about and put their needs first.

Still a little tired from the previous day's events, my dad was soon dozing while my mom and I chatted quietly. When Cam texted me and my mom asked what was going on between us, I tried to answer her truthfully.

"We've talked over everything that happened in high school. Turns out, I got a few things wrong; he never cheated on me."

"That makes a lot of sense," she said plainly. "That boy was so in love with you, I never understood how that could have happened."

That made two of us. At least I could finally put that mystery to rest. "Anyway, he's apologized for the way it all played out, and so have I."

Her mouth dropped open in a way that felt rather insulting.

"What? I *am* capable of apologizing."

"Capable? Yes. Likely to? Not so much." My mom looked truly shell-shocked. "So, what does that all mean? Are you two going to try again?"

That was the big question, wasn't it? "I'm not sure. I don't know what he wants."

He said in his text that he was ready to tell me, but I didn't know if I was ready to hear it yet. What if he said he only wanted to be friends? Or what if he said he wanted more and I let myself fall for him all over again and it didn't work out?

"What do *you* want?" my mom pressed.

I tried to answer that as honestly as I could. "I want the last six years back. I want to do it all differently."

Compassion flashed across her face as she put her arm around me, just as she had six years earlier on the night of my prom when I sat in my room alone, feeling sorry for myself. "How about we stick to what's possible instead? With everything that's happened and where you are right now, what is it you want?"

I tried again. "I want it to be easy, like it used to be. I want to be sure."

"Nothing in life is certain, Tonia, but when you're with the right person, it'll be easy more often than it's not." She squeezed me tighter before pointing over to my dad's sleeping form. "I don't know how long we've got, but do you think I'm going to give up a day of it because it might end someday? Not a chance. I'm going to squeeze every drop of joy out of every day we've got because when it comes right down to it, there's nobody I'd rather be with. There's no one who makes me feel alive the same way. So that's what you've got to ask yourself, Tonia: are you going to hold him at arm's length, waiting for him to mess up again, or are you going to jump in, grab the bull by the horns, and get messy together?"

I continued to mull over those words as I left the hospital and headed over to Dex's new gallery. He'd given me a spare set of keys to set up for the party that night, and as I walked in, I could only think it was a good thing he had, and a good thing I had the rest of the day off too. Dex's idea of a party-ready space and mine appeared to be vastly different. It took hours to get the place organized and sparkling, plenty of time for me to think about Cam.

On the one hand, we'd already lost six years, and if we were going to get back together, I didn't want to waste any more time. But on the other hand, if it didn't work out again, wouldn't that just be more time wasted?

My mom said no one made her feel alive the same way my dad did, and I had to admit that even when he made me furious, Cam always made me feel *something*. I had no apathy where he was concerned. I'd loved him and I'd despised him, but I'd never been indifferent.

Was that why things had never worked out with anyone else? Because I'd never had that same spark with them? Things got comfortable and I got bored. Cam was a lot of things, but comfortable, he wasn't. He did everything all the way, and he challenged me in both good and difficult ways.

The question came down to: what did I really want? Did I want easy, like I said, or did I want to feel alive?

The decorations arrived at five thirty, followed by the food, and soon, there was another knock on the door. I'd told my family to start showing up at six, so I figured it must be Laura or Billie, or even my parents, but when I opened the door, someone else entirely stood there.

"Am I in time for the party, Sugar?"

~Cam~

Catching Tonia Callahan completely off guard happened very rarely, but I had just managed to pull it off. From the look on her face when she opened the door, I knew for sure it had never crossed her mind that I might show up there that night.

She looked as beautiful as always, her soft blonde hair framing her face and those big blue eyes looking up at me, startled and uncertain, and I was more convinced than ever that I'd made the right choice in coming there. I couldn't spend one more night away from her, not if there was even a chance she wanted the same thing I did.

"How did you... who told you... what are you doing here?" she stuttered as I handed her the bottle of champagne I'd brought with me and slipped past her, taking advantage of her temporary confusion to get inside before she could stop me.

No one else had arrived yet, but they were clearly expected at any minute. Tonia had done an amazing job of imbuing the empty, slightly run-down space with a cheerful and celebratory atmosphere. Fresh flowers brightened the room, along with balloons and a congratulatory banner. Although the food was still covered, I could smell enough of the barbecued meat and corn to make my mouth water. I'd hardly eaten that day with my stomach in knots about how the night might go. I hadn't been this nervous about a woman since... well, ever, really.

Never had there been so much at stake.

Since I didn't know how long we'd have to speak privately, I got right to the point: "I came because I can't wait until Monday to say what I have to say."

Conflicted emotions played across her face, some that filled me with hope and some that didn't, but the fact that she was unsure gave me an extra push, if I needed it. She didn't seem to know what I might say, so I would lay it all on the line for her so she wouldn't have to wonder where I stood at all.

"Everyone will be here soon," she tried to protest, gesturing to the door I'd just walked through. "This isn't the best time..."

I cut her off before she could make any further excuses. "I know, and I'll be as quick as I can. I'm not putting it off though. You're going to hear me out, here and now, and then if you want me to go home so you can be with your family, I'll go. If you want me to be quick, don't interrupt. Just let me get it all out. Can you handle that?"

A hint of a smile pulled at her lips for the first time that night. "You know I have a hard time saying no to take-charge Cam."

Damn it, that didn't help. Blood suddenly diverted south when I really needed it all in my brain.

I gritted my teeth and did my best to smile back. "Then listen up, Sugar, because I'm going to tell you how it is."

Her smile got bigger, her lips twitching as I launched into my explanation.

"You sent me away last night because you thought we were being too impulsive, but if anything, I think we're not being impulsive enough. Instinct made me sit beside you in school. Intuition told me it'd be okay to kiss you out on that dirt road, and pure desire led to that god-awful first time we had sex."

She couldn't hold back her grin. "It wasn't *that* bad."

Selective memory could be a wonderful thing. "Yes, it was. You always said it hadn't been to spare my feelings, but I was there. I know just how long it lasted, and you're not supposed to be interrupting, remember?"

She mimed zipping her lips shut as she waited for me to continue.

"Where you're concerned, Tonia, my impulses have never steered me wrong. It was only when I listened to Marley and went against what my heart tried to tell me that I got into trouble. And ever since you waltzed into my office last week, my heart's been screaming at me. It's the reason why I went down to Corpus Christi, the reason I came back with you in the taxi, and the reason why I took you up to my apartment the other night even though every sensible part of my brain argued that it was the surest way to getting my heart broken all over again."

"I didn't really give you a lot of choice about that," she pointed out, and I raised my eyebrows at her, reminding her without words that she'd promised not to interject. Her lips pressed tightly together as she nodded at me to continue.

"I could have sent you away," I countered. "Believe it or not, I'm not so hard up that I would open my door to any woman who tried to seduce me. I slept with you that night because I wanted to, Sugar. Because I'd been dreaming about it for years, and somehow, it was even better than my wildest dreams."

Her lips twitched as she fought against her urge to add her point of view, but to her credit, she managed to stay quiet. She didn't need to say it anyway; even if I wasn't certain from her body's reaction at the time, the look in her eyes told me it had been just as good for her.

"I thought I was over you. I really thought I'd moved on, but when Marley kissed me the other night, she said I'd still been holding onto the idea of you."

"Wait, what?" Tonia's smile fell away in an instant. "She kissed you?"

"That's a long story, and not the point." Bringing it up might not have been the brightest move on my part, but on the other hand, I had no intention of hiding anything from her, not ever again. "The more I thought about it, especially last night after you sent me away, the more I realized she was right: I was never over you because I never completely let you go. How could I, when you've had my heart since the moment we met?"

Her eyes went to my chest, to my heart, and I placed my hand over it too.

"I tried my best to move on, and by most measures, I've been pretty successful. I've got my job and my friends and a good life here, but it never felt completely right. I never felt whole because a part of me was still with you. Over these last two weeks, I've felt just about every emotion under the sun, good and bad, but the point is that I *felt* them. I felt them with my *whole* heart, because you were there with me. And that's what I want, Tonia."

She listened to me intently, her hands going to her chest in a mirror image of my own posture. "What do you want?" she whispered, which was a fair enough question. I hadn't spelled it out plainly yet, but I intended to do it now.

"*This*," I explained, gesturing between the two of us. "I want this. I want the way that I feel when I'm with you. I want to feel whole again, all the time, even if you're raging at me and even if we're screwing things up. Because when it comes right down to it, I'd rather screw up with you than be safe and settled with anyone else. That probably means I'm crazy, and sometimes it sure feels like it, but right or wrong, that's how I feel. I went and thought about it, like you said, and that's my decision."

As I fell silent, my words lingered in the open air between us. Each of us stood there, our hands still on our hearts, mine racing so hard I could feel it on my palm as I put the question to her.

"All you gotta decide now, Sugar, is if you want the same thing too."

Chapter Thirteen

~**Tonia**~

Cam's words were such an unconscious echo of everything that had been spinning around my head all day, I could hardly believe it. He had no illusions about what our relationship was going to be like. *I'd rather screw up with you than be safe and settled with anyone else*, he said, and wasn't that the very point I'd been debating with myself?

Things might be easier with someone else, but they would never be as real, as vibrant, as intense.

Did I want the same thing? The better question would be if I had ever stopped wanting it.

Part of me had never completely let him go, and as I looked up into those deep brown eyes of his, I could see not only our past, but a future too, almost within reach.

But as I opened my mouth to reply, the gallery door swung open at the same time.

"We're here!" Dex called out, walking in with Shawna beside him and my parents close behind.

Of all the rotten timing in the world, my brother's must be the worst. My mouth snapped shut, my lips pressing together as frustration rushed through me, the same frustration I could see in Cam's eyes. As always, though, he put others' needs before his own, forcing his face into a smile.

"Congratulations, Dex."

The sight of Cam obviously took everyone by surprise, but Dex quickly offered him a smile and came over to shake his hand while looking between us curiously. "I didn't know you were coming. I hope we're not interrupting anything?"

They absolutely were, but there was no way to tell them that without explaining what they were interrupting, and the end result was still far too much up in the air to make public.

"It's your party," Cam replied, not quite answering the question. "And this place looks great."

Dex grinned as they looked around. "Thanks, although it looks a lot better now than it did the last time I saw it. I suspect Tonia might have something to do with that."

My brother stepped over to give me a hug, smelling slightly of clay like he often did when he'd been working on his sculptures.

"I feel like I've missed something," he whispered in my ear before pulling back, but I could only give him a tight smile.

"Cam's staying for the party, if that's okay."

I hadn't invited him to stay, so there was a chance he might not want to, but I didn't think that was likely. We still had to finish our conversation, and so when I said he was staying, he simply nodded in agreement.

"Of course that's okay," Shawna replied on behalf of everyone. "Everything looks amazing. Thanks, Tonia."

She looked better than she had in the hospital the last time I saw her, but as I hugged her too, I could feel once again how small she'd gotten.

Billie and Laura showed up shortly afterwards and my mom insisted we all eat before the food got cold, so we grabbed some plates and sat down in the chairs I'd arranged, with wooden crates forming a makeshift table. Cam popped open the champagne he'd brought and made a toast to Dex's success.

"To going after what you want," he announced, raising his glass into the air. "Even when it seems out of reach."

To everyone else, it might sound like he was talking about the gallery, but as his eyes came to rest on me, I knew exactly what he really meant.

As we all drank and wished Dex the best of luck with his new business, my mom called everyone's attention over to her.

"The last thing I want to do is ruin such a happy occasion with bad news, but sometimes that's life. You've got to take the good with the bad."

I already knew what she meant, of course, but my siblings all exchanged confused glances. "What's going on?" Laura asked warily.

Holding my dad's hand, my mom explained about his heart attack. There were expressions of concern from everyone but she pushed through until she'd explained it all, including the doctor's recommendations for some lifestyle changes.

"It won't happen right away, but I think we're going to have to sell the ranch and move here to the city. We'll be closer to you all, and closer for physical therapy and doctor's appointments too."

As expected, that set off a round of disbelieving chatter among my siblings, but having talked it over with my mom earlier that day, I had nothing to add. It would be a big change, but life never stood still, no matter how much we might want it to sometimes.

Billie looked over at me in surprise when I kept my mouth shut. "I can't believe you're not more upset about this, Tonia! Especially that he kept it from us."

That had always been my biggest pet peeve, but maybe I was mellowing a little. Maybe I could see why sometimes, people kept things quiet because they were trying to do what they thought was right, not simply because they didn't trust the people they were keeping it from.

To her astonishment, I simply shrugged. "He had his reasons, I suppose."

Dex gave me a curious look as well, his gaze once again moving between me and Cam, and I had a feeling he was putting things together a little too quickly considering nothing had truly been settled yet.

"Cam, can you help me with the cake?" I invited, getting to my feet. Some sugar would help to distract everyone. "It's in the back room."

He got up immediately, following me into the smaller room behind the main gallery which Dex intended to use for his workshop. My brother wanted customers to be able to come in and see him at work if they wanted to, as well as being able to both create and sell his work at the same time.

I really had bought a cake, but it wasn't the only reason I'd asked Cam to come with me, and he picked up on that immediately, closing the door firmly behind us as soon as we were alone.

"That was the longest damn dinner of my entire life, Sugar," he almost growled at me. "I love your family, but right now, I kind of hate them too."

I knew exactly how he felt. "They're not likely to change, so is their terrible timing and random requests to meet them at the hospital something you can deal with? Not just today, I mean, but in general?"

His eyes searched mine intensely, trying not to jump to any conclusions. "What are you saying, Tonia?"

He must know, he just didn't want to be wrong, so I spelled it out for him as clearly as he'd done for me. "I'm saying I want you too, Cameron Bailey. Every frustrating, cocky, irresistible part of you. No one else has ever made me as crazy as you do, good or bad, because no one's ever gotten under my skin like you do. I don't know if they ever could. You said you want this, and I do too, Cam. I want you, and I want to give this another chance."

The hope that dawned in his eyes, the desire and joy and disbelief all mingling together, was everything I could have hoped for. It meant he took my words just as seriously as I did, and when his arms wrapped around me a moment later, his kiss proved it too.

Although we'd kissed several times over the last week, starting with that drunken kiss at the bar in Corpus Christi and followed by the frantic desperation in his apartment and in the restroom at the bar last night, the kiss in the back room of the gallery felt completely different.

It felt like more than lust or need. Possessiveness was still present, but not just in a physical way. As Cam's kiss seared across my lips, he laid claim to my heart, and finally, just like he said, it felt whole again.

I felt whole again.

"Did you guys get lost?" Billie's teasing tone quickly changed to one of shock as she walked in the door and caught sight of us in each other's arms. "Oh, shoot, I didn't know... I mean, I didn't see anything..."

She tried to back away, but I called her back. "It's okay, Billie. I don't think it's a secret."

Cam quickly shook his head. "Definitely not."

She would want a better explanation than that eventually, but she accepted my word for the time being, holding the door open for us as Cam and I carried out the huge artist's palette cake I'd ordered. Dex burst out laughing at the sight of it, lightening the whole mood of the room just as I'd hoped.

Cam and I didn't say a word to each other as we sat side by side and ate our pieces of cake, but an air of satisfaction and happiness surrounded him, once that mirrored exactly how I felt inside too.

"You're all welcome to come over to our place," Shawna invited as we finished cleaning up all the food. "We can have some more drinks and chat more there."

Normally, that would have sounded great, but not that night as I glanced over at Cam. "We'll pass, thank you. Cam and I have other plans."

My not-at-all subtle siblings let out catcalls and whistles as I rolled my eyes.

"Why do I feel like I'm back in high school again?" I wondered out loud.

"Why do we all feel that way?" Dex quipped, but his smile was genuine as he clapped Cam on the shoulder. "I'm happy for you guys. Don't mess it up this time, alright?"

"I don't intend to," Cam told him.

I gave out hugs all around, promising my parents I'd help them start house-hunting if they were serious about moving to the city, and at last, Cam and I stepped outside onto the street, alone at last.

His arms were back around me almost instantly. "So, these other plans of yours," he murmured, pressing his lips against my forehead and his hips against mine, letting me feel just how turned on he was already. "Are they happening at your apartment or mine?"

~**Cam**~

The whole evening still felt slightly unreal. As much as I wanted to believe that Tonia said yes and that she agreed to give our relationship another chance, part of me was still afraid it would be torn away from us again. Every time we got close to each other over the past two weeks, something seemed to happen to push us apart again, and I couldn't let my guard down just yet.

Waiting for the other shoe to drop wasn't exactly romantic, but in our current situation, it felt realistic, at least until something convinced me this was really happening and wouldn't be pulled out from beneath me at any moment. Making love to her seemed a good place to start, and waking up beside her the next morning would be even better. I felt pretty certain she had the same thing in mind, so I just needed her to pick a location.

That same hope that was inside me, mixed with a tiny bit of apprehension, was at work in her eyes too as she looked up at me. "I think we should go to my place," she suggested. "My family already knows not to disturb us and we can ignore anyone else. Plus, we've already tested your bed out."

The memory of that night sent a shot of excitement through me, rushing through my whole body before heading straight to my groin. That night had been incredible, but the night ahead was shaping up to be even better since this time, we both knew exactly what it meant and what we wanted from it.

"Lead the way then, Sugar."

We could have taken a taxi, but her apartment was close enough to walk to, and as I took Tonia's hand in mine, I didn't mind taking the longer route. As much as I wanted the intimacy that was waiting for us, I wanted this too: the walking hand-in-hand, the time to think and feel and talk things over before our need for each other completely took over.

We talked about Dex's gallery and about her parents' plans to move to the city before Tonia brought the conversation back around to us.

"Does this kind of feel like a dream to you?" Tonia asked, her high heels tapping on the sidewalk as we walked side-by-side along the downtown streets. "Can we really just pick up like nothing happened?"

That actually wasn't what I wanted to do, and I did my best to explain that to her. "What happened is always going to be a part of our story. We can't change that and I don't want to gloss over it and pretend it didn't happen either. As painful and hard as it was, I learned from it, and I won't make the same mistakes again. We're *not* picking up right where we left off, but that's not a bad thing. Maybe we can think of everything that went before like a prequel, and now, this is where the real story begins."

"Cam and Tonia 2: Older and Wiser," she quipped, making me laugh.

"Something like that," I agreed, still grinning. "But not *too* old and wise. I still want to be young and stupid with you, Sugar. I want to take risks and not care too much what anyone else thinks, just like we did in Dallas."

The heat that flashed through her eyes told me she remembered every detail of that trip just as well as I did, and suddenly, I couldn't wait a second longer. A back alley branched off to our right up ahead, and I pulled her into it, past the dumpster that would almost entirely hide us from the street, all except our heads, and I pushed her up against the wall, kissing her hard.

Tonia's mouth met mine eagerly, not protesting in the least about our unexpected detour as her arms wrapped around my neck, her body pressing back against me just as firmly as I had her pinned to the wall.

"My apartment's only a few more blocks away," she murmured, teasing me even though her breathless tone told me she truly didn't mind.

"I can't wait," I explained. "I need a taste of you now."

As I dropped down onto my knees, thankful that she'd once again chosen to wear a skirt today, Tonia glanced around nervously. "Cam, anyone could see us."

Technically, that might be true, but the part of town that we were in wasn't particularly busy on a Friday night. Businesses were closed and there was no nightlife around. The only people on the streets were the ones on their way somewhere else, and most of them were too busy in their own thoughts to peer down mostly empty alleys.

"Then you better keep a lookout," I replied simply as my head slipped beneath her skirt. Gently, I raised one of her legs over my shoulder to give me better access and pushed her panties to one side. The sweet smell of her arousal was enough to make me salivate, and I couldn't wait a moment longer before running my tongue through her wetness.

"Fuck," came the whispered moan above me, making me grin again as her thighs clenched around my ears. "You really are crazy."

"If this is what being crazy gets me, I'll take it," I told her as I began to kiss her in earnest.

People said that smells and tastes were a strong link to memories, and I couldn't disagree. The scent of her took me back to long summer days, and her taste stirred up the way I felt then, like we had the whole world at our feet, like anything was possible.

It had been a long time, but finally, I felt that way again. With Tonia on my side, I could do anything at all.

My tongue flicked over her sensitive skin, teasing her clit and darting as deep inside her as I could go, given our current position. I was starving for her, and as good as she tasted, I already knew it wouldn't be enough. I would never be able to get enough.

"You are so sweet, Sugar," I murmured into her skin. "You give me such a rush."

Her thighs clenched again, letting me know she heard me. With her skirt still over my head, I couldn't see her, but I could hear enough of her sighs and whimpers and the way her breathing had deepened to know she was enjoying herself, not to mention the way her body reacted.

As I continued to suck and kiss and lick her, her legs began to tremble. "God, Cam," she moaned from above me as her body clenched and released, bathing my tongue in even more of her sweetness.

When I'd licked up as much as I could, I put her underwear back in place and removed my head from her skirt, straightening her out before getting back to my feet. Tonia still leaned back against the wall, her cheeks flushed and a sated, satisfied look in her eyes.

"Now, we can keep going," I announced with a teasing smile. "That should hold me for a little while at least."

The night was far from over, and Tonia obviously knew it as she took my hand and we headed back out onto the street and towards her apartment.

~**Tonia**~

Though Cam had briefly been in my apartment before, that night was the first time he could see all of it, and he looked around curiously as I took him into the living room.

"Do you want a drink?" I asked as I ducked into the kitchen to get myself some water. My throat felt a bit dry after all my heavy breathing out in the dry air of the back alley, and since I hoped to return the favour Cam had just shown me, I wanted to be a little better lubricated before I got started.

"Water," Cam agreed, sounding a little dry himself. "Please."

While I poured out two glasses, he examined the pictures on my wall, stopping in front of one from Dex's wedding featuring the whole wedding party, including him. I couldn't have imagined on that day that he would be there in my apartment, that we'd be on the brink of renewing our relationship, and that I would actually be incredibly happy about it.

"I told you that day that I was always going to be in your life," he reminded me with a smirk as I handed him his drink.

"I almost put a sticker over your face," I shot back before his ego got too big. "But now, I suppose I'm glad I didn't."

"I'm glad too, Sugar." He grinned again as he took a seat, his pants tight across his groin, and I sat down next to him. While he'd satisfied me a few minutes ago, he was obviously still in a state of anticipation, and though I did intend to do something about it, there was something else I wanted to ask him about first.

"Where do you think we would have been now if we hadn't broken up? In an alternate universe where Tonia and Cam went to prom together, what do you think happened next?"

The look Cam gave me was slightly confused. "Let's not waste time worrying about that. We can't change it now, we can only focus on the here and now."

"I know that," I assured him. "I'm just curious. Back then, how did you see our future?"

"Honestly?" He took another swig from his glass before putting it on the coffee table and turning to me. "I thought we'd be married a long time ago. I thought we might have a kid or two by now, if you wanted to. But otherwise, our lives were pretty much the same: me with an executive office, you kicking ass with your own business. The only thing missing in my life, Tonia, the only thing keeping it from being exactly how I dreamt it, is you."

That was just how I felt too. When I'd imagined my future life back in high school, I saw myself running my business, living in my downtown apartment, with Cam at my side. I definitely wanted kids too, though I wasn't quite sure just yet how that would fit in with my business. I would need to figure that out when the time came.

"So, that's still what you want, right?" I asked, needing to hear the words out loud to confirm that we were fully on the same page. "The family, I mean, and all the rest of it."

He leaned back with a grin. "Are you asking me to marry you, Sugar?"

My eyes narrowed to a withering glare. "If I was asking you, you'd know it. I just want to be sure we both know what we're doing here and there aren't any false expectations."

"You're making plans, aren't you?" he continued to tease me. "You want your whole life planned out as neat and tidy as those calendars you were showing me at work. Real life doesn't work that way, Tonia."

I knew that, and I also knew he was avoiding the question, so I raised the stakes by placing my hand directly on the stiff bulge in his pants. "If you want any help with this, you'll answer the damn question, Bailey."

He did his best to stifle the groan in his throat. "You're making it a little hard to think right now. How do you know I'll tell you the truth when you've given me that kind of incentive?"

My hand drifted lower, down to his balls, squeezing just a little. "Because I know you're smarter than to lie to me again."

He gave an amused, but slightly nervous laugh. "Fair enough." Taking my hand, he removed it from his groin and leaned over, kissing me softly. "Yes, Tonia. I still want all that, and God help me, I still want it all with you. I don't think I ever stopped wanting it. If you want to take it slow, we'll take it slow. If you want to be married in a month, I honestly wouldn't object. Now, for the love of all that's holy, can I please take my pants off?"

His earnest and desperate tone made me giggle, and I gave in, sliding off the couch and onto my knees on the floor in front of him. Cam's eyelids were heavy as he looked down at me.

"You don't know how many times I've dreamt about this."

"I have a feeling reality will be even better," I teased, undoing his pants and pulling them down as he raised his hips to help me. We'd had sex the other night and I'd jerked him off just last night at the restaurant, but it had been a long, long time since I tasted him and I couldn't wait to get my mouth on him again.

He was already hard and getting harder by the second as I ran my fingers lightly up and down his thick shaft. When my tongue connected with it, starting at the base and working my way slowly to the tip, Cam let out a long, deep groan.

"Fuck, Sugar, you were right. No dream is this good."

That was just what I wanted to hear, and I hadn't even gotten started yet.

My tongue pressed harder and flicked faster as I moved up and down the length of him, one hand holding his base and the other moving up his stomach beneath his shirt, at least until he unbuttoned it and pulled it off, giving me unfettered access to his firm and toned chest.

His cock twitched and stiffened beneath my touch, and when I thought he'd had enough teasing, I slowly lifted him upright from the base so that I could look directly at him while I wrapped my lips around his head and took him into my mouth.

"Shit, Tonia." He moaned out my name, his nostrils flaring and his eyes filled with lust.

Though many years had passed, I still remembered exactly what he liked, all my little tips and tricks to make him weak, learned through experimentation and repetition, and I used them all without mercy. He was helpless against the power of my mouth, just as I had been to his out in that alley, not even really caring if anyone had seen us.

But just as I was getting close to my goal, Cam grabbed hold of my head, gently but firmly, and lifted me up to kiss me. I could tell from the possessive hunger in his kiss that he was just as turned on as he looked.

"That is amazing," he promised me, his voice rough with desire. "But I need to be inside you right now. I want you there with me, coming when I say so."

My own need shot through me with those words and the firm, dominant tone of his voice, and he obviously knew it as he grinned against my lips.

"I think it's about damn time you showed me your bedroom, Tonia."

~Cam~

As incredible as it felt to have Tonia's mouth on me, it hadn't been all I had in mind for that night, not by a long shot. So, when I felt myself getting close, I stopped her and asked her to take me to her bedroom instead.

The room she led me to was impeccably spotless and organized, just like the rest of her apartment, with a very large, very sturdy-looking queen-sized bed in the centre of the room.

"That should work," I confirmed as I looked it over and Tonia smiled in both satisfaction and anticipation. My clothes were on the living room floor, but Tonia's were still on, and that was going to be a problem for what I wanted to do next. "Show me how it looks with you spread out naked on it, Sugar."

That dynamic had always worked best for us in the bedroom. Everywhere else, Tonia held her ground, but as we explored and experimented together in those teenage days, we discovered that she liked it when I took control, and I liked it too. Alone and naked was the one time I could tell her what to do without worrying that she'd take offense. She still talked back sometimes, because she couldn't fully turn it off, but in the end, she always gave in and we both loved it when she did.

That exact same mix had eluded me in all the other women I'd dated: someone who wouldn't give me an inch in the boardroom, but would take every inch when I told her to in the bedroom. In my experience, Tonia was one-of-a-kind and just my type.

As if she could read my mind, she gave me a little bit of that sass I loved. "Why don't you come over here and make me?"

Raising my eyebrows, I stepped firmly over to her and grabbed hold of the front of her blouse, ripping it open as buttons went flying across the room and Tonia gasped in surprise, her pupils dilating as her arousal grew stronger.

"You idiot, you ruined it!"

With the view I got beneath the tatters, I couldn't bring myself to care, and I didn't think she really did either. "I'll buy you a new shirt. Now, are you going to take the rest of it off, or do you want me to keep going?"

As I expected, she quickly removed the rest of her clothes and lay down on the bed as I'd asked her to.

"Fuck, Tonia, you look even better than I remember." My voice came out thick and heavy as I took in every curve and dip of her body, achingly familiar but startlingly new at the same time.

"Better than three days ago?" she challenged, even though I could see she appreciated the compliment.

"I didn't spend much time just looking at you that night," I reminded her. We had been in a bit of a hurry. "But now, I'm going to take my time."

Getting onto the bed next to her, I did just that, examining her body with my fingers and my lips. Just about every body part had a memory for me, and I shared them with her as I carried out my exploration.

"Do you remember the hickey I gave you in eleventh grade?" I wondered as I kissed my way down her neck.

"I had to wear turtlenecks for a week," she reminisced. "In the middle of June!"

"Or the first time I touched your breasts?" My lips trailed there next, finding the stiff peak waiting for me and catching it gently between my teeth.

Tonia inhaled with a shaky laugh. "I thought you were going to pass out the first time you saw them."

"Oh, that wasn't the first time I saw them, Sugar. I saw them before that, it was just the first time I got to touch them."

My tongue swirled around her nipple as I spoke, making her squirm beneath me as she tried to concentrate on what I was saying.

"When did you see them before that?" she asked in confusion, still a little breathless.

"When we were thirteen and went swimming out at the lake. You were wearing that new bikini you were so proud of and it came undone."

She raised her head to look at me in surprise. "You always told me you didn't see anything!"

I shrugged. "I didn't want you to feel embarrassed, so I lied. But that image was responsible for me having to wash my own sheets several times over the next few years."

She dropped her head again, her shoulders shaking in laughter. "You're ridiculous."

We carried on as I touched and kissed every part of her, drawing a map of our entire relationship over the landscape of her body, until I finally got to her perfect pink pussy. "This is where my very best memories are from."

"Like what?" she asked, shuddering as I brushed my fingers ever-so-lightly across her clit.

"Well, there was this one time you let me eat you out in an alley in downtown Houston."

Her laughter had only started when I sucked her clit into my mouth, my fingers sliding inside her, and both the laughing and the talking abruptly stopped. Stroking her with my fingers, fucking her firmly with them while my tongue flicked across her clit as fast as I could, I worked her into a frenzy until she almost looked ready to beg, but that wasn't what I wanted. Not that night.

Instead, I got to my knees and lined up my hard cock against her entrance, desperate to feel her from the inside again, at last, but just before I pushed in, Tonia interjected.

"Cam?" She sounded unsure, which stopped me in my tracks, though it nearly killed me to do it.

"Everything okay?"

She looked up at me curiously. "You're not wearing a condom."

She was absolutely right. "Is that a problem, Sugar?"

"It's just... you've always worn one."

It took all my strength not to move my hips, but I answered her anyway. "Well, knowing you, I'm pretty damn certain that you've got your birth control taken care of. Am I wrong about that?"

She shook her head. "You're not wrong."

"And you'd have told me if there was anything else to worry about, just like I would have told you."

Those were valid reasons, but they weren't the only reasons, and she didn't miss that fact. "Those things were true when we were in high school too, but you always wore one."

She had me there, so I told her the full truth, as I'd promised to do. "I wore one then because I didn't want anything to mess up our future. But now, this *is* our future. This is you and me, Sugar, and unless something goes terribly wrong, I don't intend on being with anyone else ever again. So, unless you have any further objections, I'm going to fuck you now like I mean it."

"You better, Cameron Bailey."

With her smile of approval, I thrust into her, finally feeling her for the first time directly on my bare cock, and it felt even better than I could have imagined. It always felt good with her, but her slick wetness and damp heat directly against my skin had to be the best damn thing I'd ever felt.

I managed to make her come twice before I couldn't wait any longer, quickening my pace until I was pistoning into her roughly, our skin slapping together as Tonia called out my name.

"Fuck... yes... you... urgh... shit." I couldn't put any words together, but she got the gist of it, and when she began to tighten around me again, my orgasm hit too, my cock pumping deep inside her, harder than I could ever remember coming before.

As I lay down beside her afterwards and she curled up against me, it truly felt like a new start. No matter how many memories we already had, there were still a hell of a lot left to make.

~**Tonia**~

Cam and I spent the whole weekend together, the first time we'd ever really been able to do that. When we were together in high school, our parents knew we were sleeping together; the secret an open one, tolerated but not encouraged. They expected Cam to go home for the night, just as his parents would send me away if we were at his house. Being together as fully independent adults was something new, and even something as mundane as making breakfast took on new possibilities when we were doing it together, arguing over which kinds of eggs were best and the right setting on the toaster to get the bread perfectly toasted.

We had gotten dressed, barely, with me in my nightgown and him wearing the baggiest pants I could find, which were still almost comically tight on him, and Cam's body pressed against mine as I fried the bacon and poached the eggs, letting me feel just how hard he'd grown again. Reaching around me, he switched the stove off, and the food went cold while he bent me over the kitchen counter, giving in to the rising need consuming us both. When we were finally satisfied, we had to start making breakfast all over again.

During the day on Saturday, we went over to his apartment so he could pick up some clothes and toiletries since he didn't plan on sleeping at his place again that night either. He told me he didn't intend to spend another night away from me unless absolutely necessary, and I believed he meant it.

Our two buildings were only about a twenty-minute walk from each other, and I could hardly believe how close we had been to each other without knowing it. If we had run into each other on the street a year earlier, would our reconciliation have happened sooner? Or did it take that particular set of circumstances - working together, him showing up in Corpus Christi, the situation with Shawna and the scare with my dad's health, Marley turning up to talk to me - to put us in the right frame of mind so that we were open to even considering it?

When I brought it up, Cam told me again that those kinds of thoughts were pointless. "The past is in the past. Let's only look ahead, okay?"

We did a lot of that over the weekend too. He wanted to know all about my business, the margins I was making and my plans for future growth, and between rounds of lovemaking in the bedroom, the bathroom and the living room, we put together a new strategic plan for A Matter of Time, based on my ambitions and his financial know-how. He told me how impressed he'd been with what I'd done at Barnly Oil, and I believed he meant it. He wasn't just buttering me up; he would tell me the truth, even when it didn't come easy.

At least I could return the compliment, since he had truly impressed me with how well he was doing for himself. I always knew he would;

that had never been in any doubt, but to see him living his dream both satisfied and inspired me. I was proud of him, simple as that.

"I've still got another two weeks of working with y'all there," I reminded him as we lay on my bed, naked, on Sunday afternoon. "Are we going public with this, or would you rather keep it quiet until we're not working together anymore?"

"It's not only up to me," he pointed out. "But if it were, I'd be shouting it from the rooftops, Sugar. I want everyone to know that you're mine."

The possessive growl in his voice sent another wave of desire through me, even though he'd just satisfied me completely. "And you don't think it'll be a problem for anyone else?"

Cam grinned at me. "Jason can't really be upset about it when he's got his own romance brewing."

He told me about how he'd found Jason and Marianne looking cozy in Jason's office on Friday morning and I shared what had happened at the bar on Thursday. For their sake, I hoped they'd had a weekend much like ours. Now that I'd fallen back in love again, I wanted everyone else to be happy too.

We agreed we weren't going to hide anything, and we spent the rest of the day looking at houses online for my parents. Cam had always had an interest in real estate too, it would have been his second choice of career, and he had a few real estate agent friends. He had no doubt we'd find my parents the perfect place soon.

"We should start thinking about where we want to buy too, Tonia. These downtown apartments are great when we're single, but when we've got kids, we're going to want more space."

He sounded so sure of us, just like always. Though some things had changed a lot, other things never would.

On Monday morning, we walked into the Barnly Oil office hand-in-hand, and though there were a few curious looks, no one made a big deal of it. My first appointment of the day was with Jason, and he asked Marianne to join us so that she could adjust her organization of his work to match the new systems I suggested. He must have thought I didn't notice how his hand slipped onto her knee under the desk, but I gave Marianne a wink when he looked away, and she blushed furiously, her face beaming in happiness as she tried to hide her smile.

"I'm so glad you came to work here," she whispered to me as we both headed out of his office at the end of our meeting.

I glanced over to Cam's office, where I could see him on the phone at his own desk, looking confident and in control. I couldn't be much happier about having come there to work too, but rather than talking about me, I focused back on Marianne. "You know, you really picked up quickly on everything I was talking about in there. Have you ever thought about being a consultant and teaching people about this kind of stuff?"

She blinked at me in surprise as we reached her desk. "You really think I could do something like that?"

"I do," I told her honestly. "With a little training and a touch more self-confidence, you'd be an amazing addition to A Matter of Time. I'm hoping to expand soon and take on some new staff, so think it over. After all, if things between you and Jason get serious, you might not want to be reporting to him forever."

My last sentence was teasing, and she smiled at it, but I could see the wheels in her head turning, letting me know she would definitely be thinking it over. When I told Cam about it later that night, back in his apartment, he gave his approval. "You should start expanding as soon as possible. I know Jason's got nothing but good things to say about you and he'll be spreading the word. You're going to be flooded with work soon. Plus, you'll want to be able to leave the business in good hands when you go on maternity leave."

His arms wrapped around me, pulling me tight to his already growing erection.

"So damn sure of yourself," I admonished him, rolling my eyes even as his certainty sent a thrill of excitement and warmth through me.

He leaned in closer. "You mark my words, Sugar. A couple of years from now, you'll be running your empire from home while our little ones run circles around you."

Those deep brown eyes had never looked so confident. "You've got it all planned out, haven't you?"

He gave me that grin that had somehow gone from charming to infuriating all the way back to charming again. "I always have, Tonia. It took a little longer than I thought, but in the end, it was always just a matter of time."

Epilogue

~**Cam**~

I proposed to Tonia one month after the party at Dex's gallery, a month after the day we decided to give our relationship another chance.

That month hadn't been all sunshine and roses; we still fought like cats and dogs whenever we had opposing views on something, but deep down, I wouldn't have it any other way, and I knew she wouldn't either. We didn't want someone who would blindly agree with whatever we said. That had never been what our relationship was about. We were both stubborn and passionate about things, but the one thing that always took precedence was our passion for each other. Every argument ended with us making up, which always satisfied me so completely, it made me want to pick a fight with her again just so we could make up again.

On that Friday afternoon, she seemed distracted when I picked her up from work at the end of the day. Her time at Barnly Oil had ended in triumph, as we both expected, and she was already on a new assignment and interviewing potential recruits at the same time. Between all that and still trying to pin down the perfect house for her parents to move into and the two of us shuttling back and forth between our two apartments, she'd been a little stressed, and it showed in the tight smile she gave me as she hopped into my truck.

"I'm happy to see you too," I teased, leaning over to give her a quick kiss before pulling back out into traffic. We had another appointment with a realtor so we had no time to waste.

"It's not you," she assured me. "I just feel disorganized, and I hate it. Organization is my thing. If we can get this house issue settled this weekend, I'll feel a lot better."

I smiled sympathetically but kept my mouth shut. I had a secret I was keeping from her that I planned to share with her later tonight, and if I didn't give too much away now, she couldn't ask me any direct questions and I wouldn't have to lie to her.

The busy downtown traffic gave way to quieter streets as we drove into a residential neighbourhood with wide, ranch-style homes, huge lawns and neat flowerbeds, with kids playing outside several of the houses.

"This is nice," Tonia murmured as she looked out the window curiously. "But the demographic might be a bit young for my parents. I was picturing more of a retirement community."

"Your dad doesn't want to feel like he's retiring," I reminded her with a laugh. "This might help to keep him feeling young."

The house we were there to see sat at the end of a quiet cul-de-sac, on a large plot with trees in the front and a huge backyard. The house dated from the 1950s but the kitchen and bathrooms had been recently redone and overall, it looked well-kept and inviting. After showing us around, the realtor left us alone to talk things over.

"What do you think, Sugar?"

Tonia looked around the bedroom we were standing in, a large master suite with its own en-suite bathroom and walk-in closet. Although it had no furniture in it at the moment, I could imagine several possible layouts. "It's great, but don't you think it's too much space for them? My mom wants to downsize and this is four bedrooms. Plus, that yard is huge, my dad's supposed to be taking it easy, not working up a sweat doing yard work."

Everything she said was bang on the money. "So, you think it'd be better suited to a young family? One just starting out?"

A smile pulled at her lips, just for a second, and I knew she could see it: *our* family within those walls. She saw it the same way I had when I saw the photos of the house online. It had been suggested as a home for her parents, but I saw something completely different when I looked at it.

Eventually, she sighed in resignation. "Yeah, it'd be great for a family, but I think we'll have to pass it on for Mom and Dad."

She started to walk towards the door, but I grabbed hold of her hand, pulling her back towards me. "What if I told you that your parents already put in an offer on a different house earlier this week, and it's been accepted?"

Her brow furrowed in confusion as my arms snaked around her waist. "Are you serious?"

I nodded. "It's only about a fifteen-minute drive from here."

She glanced around at the empty room again, still frowning. "Then what are we doing here?"

I had a feeling she already knew, she just didn't want to jump to conclusions, which made a nice change. She hadn't changed in the ways that really mattered, but I appreciated her newfound ability to hold back just a little. "Well, your parents might have found their new home, but we haven't yet."

Happiness flashed in her eyes, but she smacked my chest lightly. "Cameron Bailey, you can't take me house hunting without asking me to move in with you. You haven't even..."

She trailed off as I dropped down to one knee, pulling the ring box from my pocket. "Asked you to marry me?"

Confusion and hope and desire and outrage all crossed Tonia's face in quick succession as she stared down at me in disbelief. "You're not serious!"

Her shocked outburst made me laugh. "Do I look like I'm joking, Sugar? I've wanted to marry you ever since I laid eyes on you. Some people grow out of their childhood crushes, but I never did. I never wanted to. Even when I thought I'd lost you forever, part of me still held on, and now that you're back, now that *we're* back, I don't want to waste another minute. We might have wasted six years, but we still have a lifetime ahead of us, and I want to spend it with you. Will you marry me?"

Her eyes went wide when I opened the box to show her the ring, just as I'd hoped they would. I'd called on her sisters to help me pick out a ring, asking them if Tonia had ever said anything about the kind of ring she wanted. They had a *lot* of suggestions, and from the look on her face now, it seemed I'd nailed it.

"I secretly hoped that you would ask me to marry you at the prom." Her words took me completely by surprise, as did the tears that dotted the corners of her eyes as she looked back at me. "I know it's silly and we were so young, but I had almost convinced myself that it was going to happen. When I found out you had asked Marley to go instead, it felt like not only losing our prom, but losing that whole future too."

"Tonia." My heart broke once again as I imagined how she would have felt. She had never told me that before. All the times we'd talked it through over the last month, she'd never brought that up. "I had no idea."

"I know." Her smile flashed through her tears. "And actually, I'm glad you didn't. I'm not so glad about the rest of it, but at least now, I know that you're not asking me only because I'm the only choice you ever had. We've both tasted life without each other and we know it's better together."

She was right about that, but she hadn't said the one thing I wanted to hear yet. "Are you saying yes?" I was desperate to hear the word and get to the good part, and she laughed at my impatience.

"Yes, you crazy, ridiculous man. I will marry you."

The ring was on her finger and I was back on my feet in a matter of seconds, pulling her into a deep, lingering kiss.

"And I want this house too," she murmured against my lips, making me laugh again. "I want it all."

"We'll have it all, Tonia, I promise." Not a single doubt lingered anywhere in my mind. "No matter what came before, we've got the rest of our lives ahead of us. We're just getting started."

~~THE END~~

The Callahans

You can read about the other Callahan siblings in their own books:

A Piece of Land - Laura's story

A Change of Heart - Billie's story

A Work of Art - Dex's story

More from the Author

Contemporary Romance – 18+

Callahan Series
A Matter of Time
A Piece of Land
A Change of Heart
A Work of Art

Christmas in the City Series
Mistletoe Mistake
Candy Cane Challenge
Tinsel Temptation
Gingerbread Gamble

Charity Case

A Set of Three

Hired Lover

Contemporary Romance – New Adult/Clean

It Figures duet
It Figures
Figuring It Out

Historical Romance – 18+

Lady in Waiting Series
Lady in Waiting
King in Training
Princess in Hiding

Paranormal Romance – 18+

Cold Lake Pack Series
The Curse and the Prophecy
The Spell and the Legacy
The Dream and the Destiny

Mismatched Mates Series
Mismatched Mates
Misguided Motives
Mistaken Meanings

Serena's Story
The Alpha's Second Chance
The Returned Mate
The Vampire's Consort

Sacrifice Series
Blood Donor
Life Giver

Paranormal Romance – New Adult/Clean

The Alpha's Prey

Keep in touch

My Patreon account has daily updates from my works-in-progress, bonus chapters and more – join me there to comment and read along as my next books are being written:
www.patreon.com/melodytyden

You can find and follow me on Facebook at: facebook.com/melodyty den

Join the Facebook group Melody's Romance Corner for fun games, interaction with the author and exclusive news and excerpts.

You can also sign up to my newsletter at www.melodytyden.com for all the latest news.

Printed in Great Britain
by Amazon

22578419R00126